Tillie's Tale

BY ERLENE H. JOHNSON

ISBN: 1-55517-424-8

v.2

Published by: **Bonneville Books**
Distributed by:

925 North Main, Springville, UT 84663 • 801/489-4084

CFI | Publishing and Distribution Since 1986

Cedar Fort, Incorporated

CFI Distribution • CFI Books • Council Press • Bonneville Books

Cover design by Corinne A. Bischoff and Sheila Mortimer
Printed in the United States of America

Dedicated to new life and to those precious
little souls who have perished through
abortion or partial-birth abortion.

———

What might have been had they been
given a chance to live.

Introduction

The dismal days following October 24, 1929, Black Thursday, came to be known as the Dark Days of the Depression. It was a devastating economic period in the history of the United States. Within a few months, the production of goods began to spiral downward, causing an increase in unemployment. By 1932, approximately 12 million people, twenty-five per cent of the work force were out of work.

Countless numbers of men and boys, and some women took to riding the rails in search of non-existent work. These nomadic wanderers migrated west in the summer and south in winter time, seeking companionship and refuge in the hobo jungles that sprung up along the railroads across the country.

In contrast, the wiser families drew closer together, enduring the difficult times with careful planning, hard work and going without. They were much like a mother hen who draws her baby chicks beneath her wings for warm comfort, rest and protection. They survived together, not alone.

However, there are some of those children that were privileged to have been drawn into a close-knit family, that retain fond memories of their childhood.

It is in this period of time the following story unfolds. Although the background is in rural Utah, the town is fictional, as are all of the characters and events.

In the Thicket

November 3, 1935

*T*he thicket seemed almost barren of open fires now. The early morning sky was dark and cloudy, only a slight breeze played among the thick trees and willows. An autumn blanket with signs of an early season snow covered the temporary haven for some of the unemployed, the hobos of the depression.

The thicket offered scant protection to those heart-weary souls whose life was now riding the rails and wandering across the country in hopes of finding work, but there was no work to be found. None. They traveled mostly by freight trains, riding on an undercarriage, or if possible, in an open boxcar. Occasionally, the wandering hobos made this region an over-night refuge, a refuge which was really no shelter at all, except for the growing woods of nature. The tracks lay about thirty yards to the north of the wooded copse.

A middle-aged man and small girl were alone in a tiny clearing, neither spoke. He was clad in filthy, old, woolen pants and a tweed sport jacket, the cuffs frayed as well as the front and pockets. The collar was turned up at the back of his neck, fighting to ward off the cutting chill of the morning air. A ragged blue shirt, buttoned tightly at the neck, did little to add comfort. His gray hair, hanging well below his cap, fluttered in the breeze. Several years accumulation of body odor, dirt and smoke that had unyieldingly become embedded in his clothes, cast a rank smell. He had worn these, his only change of clothes, well past their life expectancy.

The child remained seated on the rock where he had firmly placed her a few minutes earlier. She also shivered from the cold, yet it was evident she was unconcerned with the temperature.

Her mind was elsewhere, if she had a mind. He wondered,

atally ill or orphaned, an escapee from one of those
ns" as they were called back home? Maybe it was a
me kind, but who would have time for such a charade.
't been for the blasted girl he would have been out of this
n "jungle" and on his way. Why did she have to pick him?

er attire was not suited for the crisp, morning air. The
d, cotton-print dress and a light sweater offered little
tection, as did the over-sized cowboy boots with holes in the
es. All had dirty spots of animal excretion accompanied by
alfalfa stems and leaves. She definitely carried an offensive
odor. Her filth, unlike his, had been recently acquired. Both the
man and girl were acutely aware of the other's disgusting smell.

He had hoped to be on that last freight train by now, but the
girl had suddenly appeared out of the darkness and she had been
alone. At first he thought she was with that group camped farther
down in the thicket, then he decided they had probably left
yesterday morning. Maybe they didn't. This time of the year, all of
his kind were anxious to get to the warmer climate of the south.
He didn't remember seeing any children, only two men and a
woman. He could be wrong though. The tramps didn't stay in one
place very long. It was necessary that these nomadic unemployed
constantly keep on the move to avoid being arrested for vagrancy.

This was not a major railroad line, just a small, rural, Utah,
farming community with two freights each day. The morning
one east and the afternoon one west. In this area, his kind never
ventured into town, which was located about a half-mile the
other side of the tracks. Usually, they just rested in the thicket
for a day, then moved on. He had lingered here for three days.
This was rare, but it had been rewarding due to his unexpected
discovery, a find that could change his life for the next several
months. Now, further delay disturbed him.

The child was a puzzle. Where had she come from? She
surely couldn't be traveling alone. If so, was she hoping for
someone to take her under their wing? He pondered this possibility, then brushed the notion aside. He had been aware
someone was following him, she hadn't been quiet with those
clumsy boots treading through the brush.

At first, he thought his stalker may have been another of his kind that was probably camped farther down in the thicket, someone aware of his find. He had quickly side-stepped off the path and caught her off-guard. Surprise had jolted his mind at finding his pursuer was a mere child. He grabbed and held her in a firm grip until he reached the clearing. He thought it odd that she didn't scream for help from her companions, but nothing came from her mouth. However, a rebellious battle had erupted from her feet and legs. His shins must surely be bruised.

The girl stirred. She was an odd looking child about five years old, with a very sparse growth of hair about a inch or so long. Green eyes penetrated the darkness. She had the appearance of being well-fed, whereas the little tykes in the orphanages were gaunt. He ruled the orphanage out. She must be from one of the farms, and unlike his kind, those farmers usually had enough food, but very little if any money.

Surely, someone must be looking for her. He continued pondering the matter. Last night, there had been a lot of commotion over in the village, someone may have drowned. It looked as if there was an entire army of torches searching up and down the river. Men, women and young people were calling out some name. He couldn't make it out, but it caused him some turmoil. Maybe she was the object of their hunt. Surely she must be aware of the search, and if she was the object, why didn't she let her whereabouts be known? What was with her anyway?

The sooner he left this place the better. If they expanded the search in this direction, he couldn't afford to get caught in a hornet's nest of trouble. No, not now. He had too much to lose. As he considered this possibility, an uneasiness swept through him.

Sensing her need for warmth, Norman Bello felt some compassion for the child. He bent and opened his cloth sack to retrieve a handsome, new, wool jacket. It looked as if it had never been worn and was much out of place with his other possessions. The appearance of the coat brought a sudden sharpness to the girl's eyes. She said nothing. Her eyes bore steadily into his as he slowly draped the wrapper around her shoulders. Then, he stepped back and with a sharp growl asked, "Who are ya? Where'd ya come from?"

There was only silence. Her eyes, shining through the night, reminded him of a wolf waiting at the edge of a camp, waiting to pounce on it's prey.

"What's yer name?" he asked pointedly. Again, nothing came from the girl's lips. "What's the matter, the cat got yer tongue? Why was ya followin me? What da ya want?"

Norman was taken aback when she finally did reply. "I came for the wooden box and other things." A coldness invaded the pit of his stomach, but only for a moment before he grasped control of his sudden apprehension.

"I don't know nothin about a box."

"You're lyin, you got the box. It was with this coat. I came for them." She shouted, and her well-grounded determination sparked his defensive.

"Yer crazy! I ain't got no box." He flung his words at her.

"You've got the things. I've got to have em, so as to take em back and make things right." Her voice raised, and reflected a hidden, unfaltering, bridled strength, which was much out of character for one so young.

The child's audacity brought him a few steps closer. Now he was face to face with the little chit. The eyes never left his, but for the first time, he became aware that she had recently been beaten, with a black eye, a cut along one cheek and a bruised chin.

As Norman looked at the girl, he thought of his infant son and what might have been. Eric would have been fifteen years old now. His wife, Elsie, had died in childbirth, and so had the baby. Many times, Norman felt relief that his dear Elsie and son had passed from this life and not been reduced to existence in the "hobo jungles" that had erupted since the big crash in twenty-nine. He had been laid off at the factory in the spring of thirty-two. For three and a half years he had been one of the unemployed homeless.

He remained mystified by the little vagabond. Feeling some-what more compassionate toward the girl, he reached into his sack and recovered a stale, hard cookie and handed it to her. She held the sweet close for inspection, decided it was okay, and commenced to gorge it into her mouth. Only the crunching sound, intermingled with the hooting of an owl, broke the stillness of the early morning. It was obvious she hadn't eaten in some time. Now, both seemed more conciliatory.

Norman knelt by the side of the girl and said in a brusque voice, "I said, I ain't got no box." Then, in a quiet, gentle tone he asked again, "Who are ya, where did ya come from? Do ya have a family? Ain't yer Mummy wonderin where ya are? I think ya'd better be hightailing it back ta where ya came from. There ain't nothin fer ya ta take back."

"I know you have the box. The cookies were with the box and coat, so I know you have the box too. I need everything. I can never go back until I have them. Never!" A replay of commitment burst forth in her words.

Norman was impressed by the firmness in her answer, while the green eyes, reminding him of the coyote cry earlier, slightly unnerved him. A moment of silence passed between them.

Patiently, Norman asked again, "Who are ya, where did ya come from? How do ya know about the box? We ain't gonna talk about the box no more, till I know all about ya, everything, where yer from, yer family, who beat ya, why ya stink like a —barn, everything ya remember, right down ta yer teeth. Ya hear? Understand? After that, then we'll see what needs ta be done." He paused a moment, then continued, stressing each word loudly and more distinctly. "But Ah want ta know everything."

"Everything?"

"Yeh, everything ya remember, right from the first."

The girl nodded, confirming cooperation, yet retained her guarded position and slowly began to speak. "I remember..."

Their attention was suddenly diverted by the rustle of bushes behind them. He turned, sharply alert, trying in vain to focus on the large figure in the shadows. The crackling of dried branches and sticks accompanied by heavy foot-steps was the only sound. They waited in silence as a dark form worked it's way through the trees toward them.

Trembling with fright, the little girl continued to stare ahead. She had been aware someone was following her soon after she entered the thicket. This had sparked a trembling fright inside her. Knowing full well the importance of what she had to do, she had called on her seed of courage and forced it into her soul. Thus, her fear had been trampled into the background for that moment as she concentrated on her mission.

Norman tried in vain to make out the image. Finally the form came into view. It came closer and closer. Norman was holding his breath, waiting, as a large woman emerged from the trees into the clearing. Still, shaking with fright, the child did not turn to look at the newcomer. There was no fear emanating from the woman, only an aura of strength and determination.

Her right hand, hidden in the fold of her coat, held an object, a weapon of some kind. A slight breeze whisked the fold aside, revealing an unusually large pipe wrench. Whatever her mission, she meant business.

The woman stopped at the edge of the glade and surveyed the two apparent tramps. Her first glance was at the girl, then her eyes bore into Norman's entire being. She was menacing.

He had never seen the woman before. She held no resemblance to the girl, and appeared too old to be the mother. He hadn't seen her among those riding the rails or camping in the thickets, but maybe he was mistaken. He was always aware of the women and children living in the open. His own Elsie and Eric would never have survived this life.

A protective sensation, dormant and long at rest, awoke with a sudden start. Norman immediately realized the woman had the advantage. Even though large, she moved quickly and appeared to be nimble on her feet. With an imperious hold of the wrench, she could be a serious threat to both he and the child. Quick thrusts with the wrench could crush both their skulls.

Trying desperately to remain calm, he moved to place himself between the dark figure and the girl. He raised his right hand in the air, indicating peace. To his surprise, the woman retreated to a nearby rock, and stood watching the girl. The child still did not look at the newcomer.

The three remained motionless. Moments later, the little one once more began her tale. At first, her voice was timid, but after a few seconds, she relaxed and settled into her story.

The Tale Begins

I remember the day I was born. Mama says I shouldn't tell fibs. But really, I do remember! It was on a cold, March, spring day in 1930, a Saturday.

After breakfast, Daddy and my older brothers, John and Leland, went out to the lambing shed to look after the sheep. Some of the ewes were lambing.

I was anxious to get out of that warm, little chamber inside my Mama. When the breakfast dishes were cleared away, the old, Maytag washer was rolled in from the back porch. Mama spent the morning washing and cleaning.

My sister Charolette was seven years old at the time. She had been helping Mama with the dusting and hanging the clothes outside on the line. The wash consisted mostly of baby clothes and flannel diapers. They were preparing for my grand entry into the world which was supposed to be the second week of April.

Beverly was trying to fold the freshly laundered diapers. She was five. Mama had made two dozen new ones, and there were almost two dozen old ones that were hand-me-downs from Beverly. As she sat on the couch folding them, I could hear her boasting cause she felt she was making a grand offering to help keep my bottom covered with her hand-me-downs. That wasn't so grand; she would have died of shame if she would have had to wear those diapers herself.

After the house cleaning and washing, Mama started cooking supper. I could smell fried chicken and fresh-baked bread. There were also other aromas mingled together.

I got so impatient thinking about being a part of the exciting world outside of Mama, I started to twist, turn and kick my legs. This may have troubled Mama somewhat. It was about this time that Mama suddenly sat down in the old wooden rocker situated next to the cook stove. Slowly, she doubled over as far as she was able. This kind of cramped my style. I took a dive toward the little canal. It was quite narrow. I didn't know whether to head on out or retreat back to my comfort zone.

Mother tried sitting up straight, slightly arching her back,supporting it with one hand and rubbing her tummy with the other. She was having the pains.

When they eased up she said, "Charolette, go fetch your father. Tell him the baby is coming and the pains are close."

"Beverly, you run to Emma Olsen's and tell her my time has come."

Emma Olsen is the town mid-wife. She does all the doctoring and delivering of the babies in our town. She delivered all Mama's babies. First John, then Leland. He was a Christmas baby nine years before me. I think him being born on Christmas has special meaning and before he left heaven, Jesus must have touched him with a little extra goodness. After Leland came Charolette, and two years later Beverly arrived. I was the last of the herd. Emma is proud of the other deliveries, but thinks I am Mama's great trial of life.

Beverly became extremely excited about Mama's laboring process. She not only fetched Emma to the scene but she also assumed the role of "town crier." Mama was a little embarrassed when she later heard about Beverly's hightailing it through town, shouting the news. Beverly bounded out of the house at the speed of lightening, and running past Grandma Paterson's house, she shouted, "Granny, the baby's coming! Mama hurts a lot!" She never missed a step but kept right on running toward Emma's.

Granny P. as I call her, is hard of hearing so she just kept on knitting the baby shawl she had been working on since the last October. She was still grossly involved with her needles when Lucille Evans, who lives clear through the block over on Evans road, came to the front door. Lucille likes to be well informed on everything happening, so she can spread the word. She feels that is her big mission in life. To be truthful, I think she got confused on the importance of spreading the gospel and spreading the gossip.

Anyway, Lucille came over to ask Granny P. all the details. She had heard little blabber mouth Beverly announcing the news. Of course, Granny P. hadn't heard a word, so Lucille happily related a news preview like they do at the movie house. The minute Granny P. was informed that I was in transit and Mama hurt real bad, she dropped those long needles, grabbed her old, winter shawl and headed out the door toward our house to oversee the whole process.

————

Meanwhile, Beverly continued her run down Center Street past the Post Office, then Anderson's Red and White market, on between the gas pumps at the Shell service station, all the while shouting, "Mama's having a baby. She hurts real bad."

There are always about a half dozen men hanging out at the station. Usually those feller's without a job, and nothing else to do but while away the time. Sly smiles immediately appeared on several of the men's faces followed by a comment from Joe Peterson, then laughter. Beverly was certainly spreading the word. If Mama had been aware of Beverly's broadcasting, she would have sent me back for another three weeks and made me wait until my proper birth time.

Now that Beverly had passed the business district, she turned and proceeded south on First West, still shouting the news. As she journeyed along First West, she was becoming slightly hoarse. She paused at Granny Swensen's gate long enough to relay the message in a coarse, raspy voice, then on to Aunt Ethel's. Again the grand message was cried out but in a squeaky sputter.

Emma lives two doors south of Aunt Ethel. When she reached Emma's house, she collapsed in exhaustion on Emma's front step. All she could utter was, "Mama, baby." Let's face it, the entire community had been alerted that I was on my way and had caused Mama a great deal of hurt. Some people say I've never stopped causing Mama pain.

Emma took her little black bag from the closet shelf, her shawl from the hook on the inside of the door, and promptly made her way toward our house. Emma came from the east and speaks different from the rest of our town. She uses proper English and pronunciation. Emma walks with a quick, authoritative step. All this is to prepare all those concerned at the birthing scene that she is in full command. This is to also assure any doubters that she is a skilled professional in her trade.

Meanwhile, back at the ranch, Daddy came running from the lambing shed to help with a different kind of birth; mine. The sheep would have to make do with John's assistance, Leland couldn't help, cause he had gone over to help Grandpa Swensen earlier in the afternoon.

———

Once in the house, Daddy hurriedly washed up, stoked the fire and put several containers of water on the stove to be ready for Emma. Charolette helped by preparing clean linen.

How do I know all this? While I was inside my mama, I could hear the things going on around her. That's why I was so excited to be born. I knew what kind of family I would be living with. Life was going to be a lot of fun.

One time I even heard Daddy say he wanted another boy. Mama said that would be nice but she would love me no matter what. Daddy admitted he would too. When I mentioned this to Mama, she got a funny look on her face, turned pale and left the room. I didn't get a chance to tell her about some of the other things that I knew about.

Granny P. was the first to arrive. Immediately after her, Emma came bustling through the door, all business and ready to execute her delivery powers. She started barking orders to Daddy and he started jumping just like a school boy. I guess that was because he loves Mama.

Next, Granny Swensen and Aunt Ethel landed with their knowledge and instructions. After coming face to face with Emma, they immediately retreated to the kitchen and commenced to finish what Mama had been unable to. Emma would book no nonsense from interfering relatives. When Beverly returned, her hysteria was gone. As she sat on a chair watching Aunt Ethel and Granny Swensen fix dinner, she almost seemed normal.

Maybe all the commotion made me a little nervous about changing the location of my living conditions. I knew how things were inside Mama's womb, but it started to sound scary outside. Granny P. was the only calm one. Yes, she kept her cool even while Mama was having a lot of hurt and crying some of the time. No! I changed my mind. I wasn't going to leave. I would stay put. Then I could hear Emma telling Mama to push, bear down. I refused to have Emma order me out.

I grabbed onto the wall of Mama's chamber and held tight. Emma continued to tell Mama to push and bear down. I could hear Mama cry. Emma was starting to make me angry for treating Mama that way. Maybe she could boss my family, but I was having none of it, and I refused to leave. This went on for some time.

Then, everything seemed to be pulling me away from that nice place close to Mama's heart, and there was nothing I could do about it. I held on for as long as I could, but was being forced from my security. Then everything felt different. I was out! The heat of the room wasn't as comfortable as Mama's chamber. Everything felt weird.

Emma held me up by my feet and gave me a good swat on the bottom. I said to myself, "Lady, you can't make me cry. I'll show you who's boss." Another swat, but I didn't cry. She was cleaning my nose and throat and gave another smack on my bottom. I still didn't cry. I must say, she really smacks hard. She tried everything to get my motor going but I didn't cooperate. Finally, she set me down on the table, and in a muffled, contrite voice said she was sorry, but there was no hope for me. To this day she still claims there is no hope for me.

Then she returned to the bedroom to fuss over Mama. When she told Mama, Mama started a sad cry. That's a different cry from a hurt cry, or a cry to try and get your way. Daddy put his arms around Mama and held her tight.

Granny P. came over to the table, picked me up and wrapped me in a warm, flannel blanket. She placed me, blanket and all, in a little box, opened the oven door and shoved me inside. She left the door open. When Beverly saw Granny put me in the oven, she burst into tears. Thinking Granny had not only lost her hearing but her eye sight as well, and had mistaken me for a roast or something, Beverly tried to pull the box out. Granny P. gently stayed Beverly, telling her that I would be alright. I wasn't baking.

While I was basking in the heat of the old, black and white cook stove, Granny pulled the rocker chair near the oven and started to sing a cradlesong. The soft melody started to lull me out of my fright and stubbornness. Granny Swensen and Aunt Ethel paused from their kitchen fussing to come and fuss over me by massaging me.

It was starting to get really too hot for me. I wasn't used to that kind of oven, so I opened my mouth, took a gasp of air, then let out a wail that shook Emma off the balls of her feet and brought a rush of happy tears to Mama's eyes. Emma came rushing into the kitchen, scooped me up in her arms, then returned to the bedroom where I was placed into Mama's soft arms. Daddy was sitting next to the bed. They both seemed to be a little teary-eyed.

At the time, Emma referred to me as Gwen's darling, little angel. It was the only time Emma Olsen ever thought I was an angel. Sometimes she acts like if I hadn't been "baked," Gwen Swensen's life would have been much simpler, but Mama loves me and knows I'm a special gift from God.

A "Big" Mistake

*O*f course, right after my birth, Mama was in bed for a long time. Daddy rocked me that first night and continued right on till I got big enough to be mortified by the sissiness of the whole thing.

A few days later, after Mama was able to get out of bed, she wrapped me in the new baby shawl that Granny P. had finally finished and took me to church to be blessed with a name. I was named Matilda Faye Swensen. Matilda after Granny P. and Faye after Granny Swensen. This was very upsetting. Mind you, I love both my grannies, especially Granny P. She baked and sang to help me get started.

When I heard the name I had been given, I started to scream as loud as I could. I tried to let them know they were giving me the wrong name. I cried so loud and long that Mama had to leave church and take me home, she thought I was sick. After two days, I was so tired, I gave up and went to sleep.

The family calls me Tillie. That's okay, but the real problem was that I should have been named Henry after my daddy. I felt Heavenly Father had made a terrible mistake, and when he realized it he would eventually fix this error. He had intended for me to be a boy instead of a stupid girl. That way I could grow up to be a cowboy just like my daddy, whom I really idolized. Yes! There had definitely been a big mistake.

Right from the start, I hated dolls and no way would I play house like Beverly and the other girls fiddled away their time. It would have been like being condemned to that awful place where the devil is said to live and no sane person wants to go!

I loved to be out-doors and play in the dirt. Even before I

could walk, I would crawl out the kitchen door and climb down the back porch steps, over the hard packed dirt path and out to the horse corral. There I would sit in the dirt by the fence and watch Daddy and some of the other men with their horses. Joe Peterson was always coming over trying to trade horses. He sure used some different words. Words Daddy never said. John referred to them as Joe's french.

Once in a while, Leland would place me in front of him in the saddle. Together, we would ride his horse Smokey to drive the cows out to the pasture. He knew I loved this, so when I was almost four years old, he and sometimes John, would saddle old Meg with the child-size saddle and let me ride along with them, but they kept close watch on me.

I loved all the happy days. They were filled with all kinds of activities. Then in the evening after all the chores were done, the family gathered around the kitchen table to savor Mama's sturdy meals.

After dinner, while Mama, Charolette and Beverly cleaned up the evening dishes, Daddy would rock me in the old, wooden rocker. At first, this rocking business would commence after Daddy had his after dinner smoke. He used the roll-your-own, Bull Durham tobacco and the little, white tissues. I would sit on his lap and try to grab that enticing, little, white thing out of his mouth. Of course, he would say no, no. Finally, I just gave up for the time being and did the pretend business of rolling my own and then puffing away. Daddy thought it was cute the way I mimicked him.

After our evening smoke, his real and my wishing, I would don a pair of Leland's old cowboy boots, put on Daddy's big, tall, pointed, cowboy hat and clomp around the kitchen pretending to be a big man just like my Daddy. Charolette and Beverly thought I was weird, cause I hated dolls and tried to act like Daddy, but I was really practicing to be a cowboy, so when Heavenly Father fixed his mistake, I could just go right on with my life. I would already know what to do.

Joe's French

One day just after my fourth birthday, I had on Daddy's hat and Leland's boots. The boot tops came clear up to my thighs, and I had to shuffle along the ground to keep them on my feet. My dress covered the tops. I wandered out to the corral. Joe Peterson and two other men were out there trying to trade a horse to Daddy for old Meg. Daddy said no, that he wanted to keep Meg for me. He said Meg was a good horse for kids.

While the men were talking, Joe's little black and white sheep dog took after one of our ewes. Joe hollered at the critter. "Get back here you little bastard!"

Strange, I thought the dog's name was Flea. When Joe kicked his dog, the gray horse he was trying to trade to Daddy started to back away, chomping at the bit, front feet leaving the ground. Joe started hitting the horse with the reins, then he called the horse the same name he called his dog!

Daddy looked at Joe with a glare, like he didn't like the way Joe was acting. Joe turned on Daddy and said that Randall Anderson was a cheat and called him the same name. This really surprised me that the dog, horse and owner of the Red and White Market all had the same name. Mr. Anderson must have changed his.

Just then, somebody grabbed me up and lifted me up in the air to tote me back to the house. It was Leland. He said I shouldn't be out where Joe Peterson was because he had a dirty mouth. Heck, I knew that already. I've seen Joe spit. He's always spitting, trying to clean all that dirt out but it ain't no use. His spit always looks a muddy brown. Anyway, I had to stay in the house while Joe was outside. I didn't like that because everyone in the house was doing stupid girl things.

Beverly wanted me to play house but I wouldn't. I just sat down and pretended to have a cigarette.

Two days later, things kind of came to a head when Mama had to go to the market and trade some eggs for fabric. She said I could go if I stayed in the car.

Grabbing Daddy's "big ten gallon" hat and Leland's old boots, I immediately climbed into the back seat of the car. Daddy had a package of real, ready-made, store-bought cigarettes sitting on the front seat. I thought that was nice. They were the Lucky Strike brand that came in the green packages. They were prettier that the home-made ones.

When we got to the store, Mama told me to wait in the car, she would only be a few minutes. The Mamas of this world sure have long minutes. I could see her through the window. She was talking to some other women. There was Emma, the spanking midwife, Lucille Evans and her boy, Paul, who is my age. He was born three months after me. That's why he isn't very smart. Another woman named Mable Stewart had joined in with their gossip. Mabel teaches school and has big breasts. I waited and waited. Mama hadn't even begun looking at the fabric.

Well, I would just take one of Daddy's Lucky Strikes and wait. I plopped a nice, fresh one into my mouth. I felt like I was king of the ranch.

Granny P. came wandering down the street, then seeing Mama in the store with the other women, she opened the door to join the group. Now they all had to say every word twice so Granny P. could hear. This was going to take forever. Mama needed a reminder that I was waiting.

As I climbed out of the car, both boots fell off my feet. Upon reaching the ground, I replaced them and shuffled toward the store entry. Decked out with hat, boots and a Lucky Strike dangling from my mouth, I could barely push open the heavy door.

Once inside, I let the door shut with a bang. Emma was the first to see me. Her mouth flew open. It's a funny thing, her upper teeth came flying out of her mouth. I didn't know people could take their teeth out. Grandpa Swensen doesn't have any teeth to take out. Her's fell on the floor. She hurriedly bent over to recover them before anyone saw what happened. Mama and the other ladies hadn't noticed me or the short trip Emma's teeth had taken. Only Mr. Anderson seemed to be aware of me now, so I walked to the counter, looked him straight in the eye and said, "Hello you old, cheating bastard." I used the name that Joe calls him. I thought he would be happy to know that I was smart enough to know his new French name.

Mr. Anderson stopped what he was doing and glared at Mama, then at me. Mama must have recognized my voice, cause her attention was no longer on the idle chatter coming from her friends. They all stopped talking and gawked at me. Mama closed in on me fast and quick. I thought she must be sick, her face was so red.

Paul Evans peeked around his mother's skirt and pulled a face at me, then laughed. Mama yanked that cigarette out of my mouth, and whipped me up and out of that store so fast the boots and hat went flying. Granny P. stooped to pick them up. All the ladies looked surprised that I knew how to smoke and I was only four years old. There wasn't a single grown-up lady in the whole county that could smoke.

There was no fabric for new dresses that day. Mama must have forgotten it.

She put me in the car, then headed for home. I could see her shaking her head and tears running down her cheeks. I wondered what I had done to upset her.

When Mama drove into the yard, Daddy was walking up the path from the corral. She got out of the car and ran to him. I could hear muffled words. Every little while Daddy would look over in my direction. Mama was crying, then Daddy put his arms around her. They stood there hugging each other. Mama just didn't know what to do. I think she thought I was a problem. That was the first bad day I had ever had since Emma had announced that I was an angel. I somehow knew I hadn't done the work of an angel.

There wasn't the happy chatter at supper that night. The conversations were more strained. After the meal, Daddy didn't have his usual smoke. He came over and picked me up in his arms, gave me a nice hug, then went over to the kitchen stove and put his tobacco and Lucky Strikes into the fire. He stood there holding me in his arms so I could see too. He said there would be no more smoking. We were going to do different, fun things together. He said smoking was a bad habit, then he took a book from the shelf and walked back to the old wooden rocker and sat down.

Daddy said we were going to change a few things at our house. First of all, he would not be smoking again. From now on, we would read stories in the evening and do fun things together.

That night, we set in the rocker by the stove, while Daddy read "Hansel and Gretel" to me.

It was hard for Daddy to quit smoking, so he and Mama decided it would be easier to get rid of a bad habit by replacing it with a good one. Daddy started to do wood carving. At first it was hard. I thought maybe I needed a new habit too, but couldn't think of one.

When Daddy and Mama tucked me into bed that night, Daddy explained to me about choosing the right. He said that he and Mama didn't like me using Joe's French or calling people bad names, like I did Mr. Anderson. Mama said that it makes people feel sad to be called names, and when we do naughty things, Jesus wants us to go back and make things right, then never, never do the naughty things again. I thought that was a good idea.

————

The next day, Mama took me into Mr. Anderson's store to say I was sorry. That was easy, cause I just thought he had changed his name to a French one. I would never want to make him feel sad. He's a real nice man. Before we left the store, he gave me a candy sucker. Daddy talked to Joe Peterson about some words that he couldn't use when he was on our property. The whole town seemed to know I smoked and spoke Joe's French, but I noticed that Joe didn't use his French after that, even when he wasn't on our place. He just spoke English like our family does.

The New Girl

*E*veryone said I looked like Grandpa Swensen. He was away from home most of the time, herding sheep. Grandpa didn't have any hair or teeth. I didn't have very much hair, it was short and stubby, but I had some teeth. All the other kids my age had lots of hair.

Once a month, Daddy, John and Leland went over to Aunt Ethel's. She would cut their hair for twenty-five cents. Uncle Carl died in the big flu epidemic a long, long time ago, so Aunt Ethel needed the money. She earned most of her income from curling and cutting. Since I didn't have any hair, Mama said I didn't need to go, but I always bawled until she let me tag along.

Mama sewed me a new dress and matching bonnet trimmed with lace. I think the bonnet was to cover my bald head. She was anxiously waiting for the day when there would be enough hair to wear ribbons. Mama must really want me to be a nice, pretty girl.

It was Saturday night and everyone was taking their turns in the number three wash tub. That's how we bathed. Our freshly pressed clothes were hanging in the closet readied for church. Charolette, Beverly and Mama had their hair wrapped in the little, metal curlers.

After dinner, and before the bedtime story, Leland would put his boxing gloves on me and a pair on himself. He had been teaching me to box. There was a right to the jaw, a left to the nose and a good upper cut, all the time keeping up a strong guard. We had been practicing several times a week. This was ever since we listened to the big Joe Lewis match on the radio. Leland was a good teacher and he didn't ever hit me very hard.

Then Mama said I would be wearing my new dress and bonnet to church. This really upset me. Why couldn't I wear Leland's boots and Daddy's old hat? Then the lacy dress wouldn't be so bad. No! Not to church was Mama's stern reply. I could wear them after church. Of course, I countered that Daddy didn't go to church and I wasn't going to go either. Mama and I had a clash over the whole thing. Of course, the only argument I knew how to use was tears. After raising four older children, Mama was familiar with that tactic, so I lost that round.

Dressed like a little, bald-headed princess, off to church I went. After we all climbed out of the car, Mama grabbed my hand and marched me up to where the nursery class was seated. Paul Evans looked at me in that weird bonnet and let out a sly smirk. I returned a nice, friendly, warm smile, but underneath I thought, someday I'm gonna give you a good right to the jaw. He's a coward and never fights. When I smiled, he ducked his head and turned away.

There was a new girl in the nursery class that I had never seen before. She was sitting off by herself. I said hello to her, then I went over to the other side of the bench, so I could see out the door. She acted pretty nice.

Lucy Sorenson and Sally Brown were sitting by Paul. They both stuck their tongues out at me, then looked away and laughed. They have long hair and always wear nice dresses. Their daddies have jobs and work at the school.

It was a hot, summer day. All the doors and windows were open, the mamas were using their little hand-fans to stir the stale air, the daddies were tugging at their shirt-collars and ties, and the kids were squirming in their seats. Everyone felt the heat. I looked out the door at the little stream trickling past the trees that edged the church yard. It looked cool.

Then it was time to go to our classes. I politely waited for the rest of the class to lead the way, then I followed at a brisk walk. Oh! I did look anxious. I saw Mama and Granny P. out of the corner of my eye. Mama looked proud of me. Granny wasn't impressed.

We left the chapel, then walked down the hall toward our class room. I spied a vacant bench against one wall. Looking around to make sure no one was watching me, I dashed underneath and crouched close to the wall out of sight. As soon as the hall emptied, I made a fast run out the side door, heading for the little stream and clump of trees. Upon reaching that little bit of paradise, I immediately took off my shoes and socks. I soon decided to take off the rest of my clothes. I didn't want any traces of the swim to show.

I ran up and down the creek splashing in the cool water. Then I danced and played in the mud along the edge. I was having lots of fun.

Suddenly, the double doors to the church opened and the congregation began pouring out. Mama was in about the middle of the group. There were a few comments, finger-pointing and laughter; everyone was watching me "swim." Mama left the group, and with a quick gait, headed in my direction.

There was that red face and tears again. Granny P. was right behind her. Mama lifted me out of the water and turned to look for my fancy, new clothes. While I was still dangling in mid air, I could see Paul Evans staring at my wiggling, mud-covered form trying to touch the ground. He always seemed to gleam whenever I was in trouble.

The new girl came out of the church, and when she saw me, she didn't laugh. I got the idea that maybe she would have liked to swim too.

Granny walked over to Mama and quietly said, "Gwen, I know your nerves are frayed. Calm down, take your family home and rest a bit. I'll see to the child."

Mama had just gotten to the car when Emma stopped. She looked into my eyes, shook her head and said, "You're supposed to be an angel." My word, I thought, how can I be an angel, when I don't know how? I'll need help with that.

Granny P. helped me clean off most of the mud, then I got dressed and together we walked to her house. She never said a word about my "swim." There were a few curious folk that stayed until the show was over. I think they wondered if I'd get the stick to my bottom. Daddy and Mama never spanked. Granny P. sometimes spanks a couple of swats. She thinks it makes good reminders.

At Granny's house, she found an old dress Mama wore when she was a little girl. I put it on after a really good scrub. Granny cleaned my fancy clothes. We had peanut butter and honey sandwiches for lunch. She told me stories about my mama when she was a little girl. It was fun to stay at Granny's.

The next day, Daddy gave me a good talking to. I noticed that Daddy went with us to church after that, and helped Mama a lot more with us kids.

After my Sunday swim and Daddy's lecture, I was beginning to feel like I had a pretty good handle on life. I had quit pretending to smoke most of the time, I had learned there was something called swearing that some people call French and it was a naughty language which is forbidden, and no more swimming in the raw at church. I was starting to see the direction little angels should travel.

Boys Are Different

*I*t was one, bright, sunny morning soon after my fateful Sunday swim, and I was helping Beverly dry the breakfast dishes. Charolette was washing them. I wiped the pans and silverware while Beverly did the breakables. It really wasn't so bad doing girl's work if it wasn't too often or for long periods of time. I was actually pleased with myself.

After we finished, I put Daddy's "ten gallon" hat on my head, Leland's old boots on my feet and headed for the corral. There was a man with Daddy that I hadn't seen before. As I came closer, I noticed the new girl from church was playing on my tire swing. Leland had tied an old car tire to a rope and made a swing for me. The swing was in the orchard and tied to a branch of the apple tree. I shuffled over to where she was gliding back and forth.

It was no time at all until we were friends. Her name was Sherry Allen. She had come over with her daddy. He was trying to trade a cow to my daddy for some grain. They had just bought the Holt farm.

We took turns in the swing, then ventured over to the sand pile. Finally, she said she liked my hat and boots. Then she asked why I wore them. I said that I needed to because I was going to be a cowboy like my brothers and Daddy. She told me that I couldn't be a cowboy, I would have to be a cowgirl. That really jarred my whole being. I started to cry and shout at her and said I was going to be a man. She said I couldn't because I was not made to be one. Oh yes I was, couldn't she see that I was bald just like Grandpa Swensen. She said that didn't matter. My other parts were different. PARTS? What *parts*? How? Then she revealed the shocking news that when boys went to the outhouse, they did it different. Well, I knew that was a lie because all the men and boys I had seen went in just like the girls. They closed the door just like everyone else. When they finished, they came out feeling better just like we do. So there! No difference!

Then she whispered to me how the boys were different. This was a big surprise to me. I knew that girls didn't have any parts like that.

I asked how she knew all this. She said cause she had a baby brother and she had helped her mama change his diapers.

Well, I certainly didn't want any extra attachments. I would stay just like I was. Now I liked being a girl, I just didn't like to do girl things. When I told Sherry this, she said we would grow up to have breasts like our mama's had. I wasn't happy about that either. I didn't want those things flopping around on me. Especially if they were big and saggy like Mabel Stewart's, but then, Mabel is a really nice lady so I guess it doesn't matter.

Sherry was sure smart. I was glad she had come over to play, but I was going to ask Mama about all these things.

I did ask Mama. She helped me understand a little bit more. After Mama's talk, I knew Heavenly Father hadn't made a mistake on me. I was happy with the way he had made me. He knows best.

Now I knew that the outhouse business was different for boys than for girls. Mama said that when I was big like Charolette, she would tell me some more things. Mama is smarter even than Sherry!

Mr. Sorenson

*N*ot too long after my fifth birthday, it was decided that I should have some family responsibility each day. Charolette and Beverly helped Mama with the washing, ironing and house cleaning. Charolette was eleven and was starting to learn to cook potatoes for supper and eggs for breakfast.

I wanted to take the cows to the pasture every morning after the milking. Daddy said I was too little. I used my old stand-by argument. I begged, but mostly wailed and bawled.

Leland finally suggested to Daddy that he help me until they were sure I could do it. I was relieved when Daddy agreed. That crying business was beginning to wear me out. I'd hate to be a panty-waist and use tears all the time. Girls can use tears but boys aren't supposed to.

Each morning after milking, Leland would put the little saddle on old Meg, he would mount Smokey and together we would take the cows to the pasture which was about a mile down the lane.

About five-thirty in the afternoon, we would fetch them back to the barn-yard to be milked. I loved my new job. Of course, Daddy's big hat and Leland's old boots were part of my regular working gear. Leland was fun to work with and he continued to teach me about boxing in the evenings.

One time after I had taken some milk over to Aunt Ethel's house, I passed the school yard. There was a circle of the big boys shouting and cheering. They were at least nine years old. Girls were standing around in little groups on the outside of the circle.

I ran over to see what the excitement was all about. After I crowded in between several of the boys, I ended up on the inside of the circle.

Bobby Stewart and Michael Evans were circling around each other with raised fists. Both were crying and daring each other to step over a line. They were both stepping over the line and neither one was brave enough to sock the other one. They sure weren't very good fighters. I joined the big boys in encouraging a few blows.

It wasn't long before Michael's mother, Lucille Evans, who teaches second grade, came on the scene. Mr. Sorenson, the principal, was right behind her. Mr. Sorenson is mean to all the kids and rude to the adults who haven't been to college. He also bullies all the women teachers. Once, a long, long time ago, I heard Joe Peterson use some of his strange language and then say Mr. Sorenson was a jerk.

They put a stop to the fuss real fast. Lucille saw me and told me to go home, I was too little to be there. I didn't move fast enough and mean, old Mr. Sorenson grabbed me underneath the arm. He hoisted me right out of my boots and gave me a good shaking. Both my hat and boots were on the ground. When my feet hit the ground, his hand hit my bottom with a good swat.

Mr. Sorenson told me to get off the school grounds and not to come around starting trouble. He also said I should dress like a lady instead of wearing some kind of dirty, old boots and hat. He used another word that I wasn't familiar with, but knew it was part of that forbidden language.

I decided to take the long way home and go down the lane past Sherry's house. As I was shuffling along through the dusty tracks, I saw a large, dead snake. It had been run over and hadn't been dead very long. I had seen snakes before when Leland and I drove the cows so I knew what it was. This snake must have been a baby cause it had a rattle fastened to it's tail, but it was way too big to be a baby. I took off my hat, then picked enough grass from along side of the road to line the inside. I carefully put the long skinny fellow inside the crown.

When I reached Sherry's house, she was on the grass playing with her cat. I showed her my new snake. Then I told her about the fight and Mr. Sorenson. We talked about it for a while, then headed for the school. I took off my boots so no one would recognize me. Of course, I was already carrying my hat with Slinky Sam in it.

When we reached the grove of trees just across from the back entrance of the school, we ducked down in the under-brush. We laid flat on our tummies and watched all the movements across the street.

The kids were coming out of the big doors. School was out for the day. The teachers usually stayed about another half hour and then Mr. Brown, the janitor, would be the only one in the building. Mrs. Stewart, Bobbie's mother was the last teacher to leave. She teaches first grade.

We waited until Mr. Brown began cleaning the class rooms in the rear of the building. He usually did those last. Barefooted and crouching low, we raced to the big double doors in front. We crossed the hall to Mr. Sorenson's office. The door was unlocked. Very quietly, we crept inside and closed the door again.

On the desk was a large piece of paper with a lot of writing on it. We both bent over it and commenced picking our noses. It wasn't long until blood was coming from our nostrils. We let it drip onto the paper. When the blood stopped, we picked again until we had a nice pool of blood. Sherry said she could write, so she dipped her finger in the blood and wrote: U R DED. We daubed the blood over most of the paper. Now for Slinky. We coiled the snake up as best we could and dripped blood on his head, then turned to leave.

Suddenly, we could hear footsteps and doors closing. Some one inserted a key into Mr. Sorenson's lock. Snap! The door was locked. Sherry and I looked at each other. We were imprisoned in the principal's office. We were doomed. Slam! The front doors closed for the night. Mr. Brown was leaving. No one would be coming to the building until Monday morning. Maybe we would die and our mama's wouldn't know where we were.

We both ran to the door and tried it. No luck. It could only be opened with a key from the outside. There were two other doors in the room. The first one opened into a closet. We rushed to the second door. It was unlocked. Excitedly we opened it. It opened into a small room, the supply room. The walls were lined with shelves filled with supplies. If we were going to die in this place, we could color with some of the crayons and paper while we waited for the end to come, but first things first. We checked a door on the end of one wall. It was locked. No luck there. We went back into Mr. Sorensen's office and sat on the floor by the door and started to cry. After a minute or two, it was obvious that crying was a waste of time. No one could hear us. Besides, it made us tired.

We sat there looking at the row of windows and wondered if we could reach them. We pushed Mr. Sorenson's chair over and climbed up on the ledge. We started to go right down the whole row. The second from the last was unlocked. It took both of us lifting to get it open. I ran back to Mr. Sorenson's desk and grabbed my hat. Now we were free to go.

It was a long jump from the window to the ground. We knew we could either jump or die together in Mr. Sorenson's office. I didn't mind dying with the snake, but after Mr. Sorenson swatted my bottom, I would rather leap to my death than stay in his room.

Well, we both jumped to the ground and it didn't hurt either of us. We ran back fast to the grove of trees to get her shoes and Leland's boots. That was when we saw him. He had seen us coming through the window. We were caught and would maybe go to jail.

Paul Evans was playing over by the stream near the trees. We knew he would love to tattle on us. We covered our bare feet and beat it over to where he was.

Right away he wanted to know what we were doing in the school. I spoke up and said we were doing work for the angels and it was a secret. His eyes got big when I said angels. Then Sherry told him the destroying angel would suck the blood from anyone that told on us. He wanted to know if that was why we had blood on our faces. We looked at each other. I said no. I said the angels put it there to protect us from harm and since he had seen it, if he told even his mama, he would catch on fire and die.

Paul started to bawl really hard. We had to stop those tears, so we told him that as long as he kept this secret and wouldn't cry, he could play in my sand pile for two hours every Friday afternoon. Paul didn't have any friends or a sand pile, so he was happy about that.

We told Paul goodbye and reminded him he could play with us in the sand pile next Friday, then washed our faces in the ditch.

Sherry said it would be safer if we separated to go home. Sherry sure knows a lot of things.

When I passed the Red and White Market, a strange car was parked out front. A tall man wearing a white shirt and tie was talking to Mr. Anderson. A woman was standing close to Mr. Anderson. Her arm was linked through his. She leaned over, kissed him on the cheek and said, "Don't worry Dad, we'll be back next week. We'll help you."

The lady was Mr. Anderson's daughter, Susan. She and Mama were friends when they were young girls. I stopped to watch, then a boy came out of the store. He was about my size. He had dark hair and big, chocolate, brown eyes. He sure looked clean and nice. He didn't even notice me. All of a sudden, I wished I was pretty and had lots of hair.

That night at dinner, Mama said Mr. Anderson was having serious health problems. Susan and her family would be moving back to town to help with the store. Mama was going to help Mr. Anderson in his store until Susan's family arrived. Daddy said Joe Peterson was ailing too. He had been down in bed for a week. Mama said Joe has had a hard time and had let himself go, ever since his heart was broken. I thought maybe he should go to Emma and get it wrapped up like Clay Oliver did when his arm was broken, but didn't say so. I'm not sure what part holds our hearts.

After Daddy read "Goldilocks and the Three Bears" to me, he started to do his whittling. Mama had a sewing basket full of stockings with holes in them. She was darning the heels so we could wear them some more. Charolette was embroidering a dish towel made out of a flour sack, and Beverly was playing with her paper dolls. John and Leland were trying to put a puzzle together. I got Mama's hair brush and started to brush my fuzzy head. Mama gave me a nice smile.

Joe's Stink!

Joe Peterson didn't seem to get any better. Leland went over every night and morning and milked Joe's cow. Mama sent some fresh baked bread and soup over with my daddy. Mama was busy helping Mr. Anderson everyday until Susan and her family arrived.

Joe didn't have any family. He was all alone. No one to tuck him in bed or read him stories. When I was sick, all Mama's fussing over me is what made me better. Beverly and I were home alone. I told Beverly that Joe needed to know that people cared so he could get better.

I pushed a chair over to the cupboard, pulled myself onto it, then climbed onto the counter top. I was able to reach the peanut butter and honey. The slices of bread I cut weren't pretty and even like Mama's, but the peanut butter and honey sandwich was a masterpiece. I wrapped it in some newspaper that Emma Olson gave to our family. She takes the paper and brings it over to our house when she is finished reading it. That way, we get to read about what President Roosevelt is trying to do about something called the depression.

I tucked the sandwich into an old, shoe box and asked Beverly to help me make a card for Joe, cause I didn't know how to write.

I drew a picture of a cowboy in bed with his hat and boots on. I told Beverly that nobody loved Joe. She said that Heavenly Father loved him. She wrote on the card that God loved Joe and that I loved him, and then she signed my name.

I put the card in the box with the sandwich. I found some pretty, yellow dandelions and put them in the box too, then added the little rose that was on Mama's bush. Off to Joe's I went with the magic, get-well box.

Joe was sitting in an old, dirty, rickety chair on his front porch. He looked white and his hair was messed up. I don't think he had combed it all week. He just had ragged pants on and a undershirt. If he was my daddy, Mama would make him take a bath. His front door was open and flies were buzzing all around. A strong, icky stink was coming from inside his house. He hadn't cleaned up any of his messes.

He looked at me and said in a grouchy voice, "What do you want kid? Go on home! I don't want you around here." I told him I had a magic box to make him well, and I set it on his lap. He lifted the lid, took out the card and read it. He looked at it for a long, long time. I guess he never had a card before. His eyes got a little teary like Mama's do sometimes. That must come from being grown-up.

I told Joe I had come over to help him get well. He said it didn't matter if he ever got well. Poor Joe sure sounded sad. Joe needed a mama to take care of him and I told him so. He said there ain't nobody that wanted him. I said maybe Emma Olson. He laughed an awful laugh and said she was almost old enough to be his mother. I thought, that's fine, that way she could do a better job.

I left him sitting in the sun on the porch and went into his house. It was sure dirty and smelled like spoiled food and mice.

I knew how to sweep floors, so I did that. There was an old, dirty, dish towel on a chair, so I used it to dust. Dishes with moldy food were scattered all over. I tried to do the dishes by standing on a chair. Things began to look a little better.

When I went back out to the porch, Joe was still in the chair. I told him that Heavenly Father loved him and wanted him to get well and be happy. He just looked at me and said thanks, then I went home.

The next night at dinner, Daddy said Joe was doing a lot better and had cleaned up a bit. He had even taken a bath.

The Threat

Beverly was real excited when she came home from school on Monday. Someone had broken into the school. They had left a bloody note threatening to kill Mr. Sorenson with a rattlesnake. Beverly said the snake had died over the weekend, waiting for Mr. Sorenson to come to school.

Mr. Sorenson thought it was one of the students that had made the threat, but Clay Oliver, the cop, thinks it was one of the former pupils that still hates Mr. Sorenson. Clay said he would find out who it was and put the dirty ba... in jail.

Mama interrupted and scolded Beverly for almost using that word. I suddenly felt too sick to ask about what the word was that she didn't quite use and I'm not supposed to know.

I took three cookies from the jar and headed for Sherry's house. I thought we had better visit Paul and share a cookie with him. He could even play in the sand pile before Friday.

———

Paul could tell we were nervous. He started to be a little braver than he had ever been before. He wanted our cookies too.

We said no, we were going to eat our cookies. He started to cry and said he would tell who was in the school.

I gave him a good, strong upper-cut to the chin, then a quick left to the nose. Blood started shooting from his nostrils and ran down his face.

Sherry told him that the angel gave me power to make the blood come and this was just a warning. If he told on us, blood would come from all over his whole body. That made him cry even harder.

Paul looked a mess and he was frightened, so we helped him stop the bleeding and washed his face in the ditch. He didn't like that, he wanted clean water, his mama always keeps him nice and clean, but he promised not to tell on us.

We didn't hear any more from Mr. Sorenson and Clay about the bloody note. I thought they must have forgotten about it.

Susan and her family finally arrived to help Mr. Anderson. The daddy's name was Harold. The nice-looking boy with the big, brown eyes was Roger Benington. He came to church on Sunday. Sally Brown and Lucy Sorenson ran to sit by him. He didn't even look at me and my ugly bonnet. Sherry and I sat on each side of Paul. Paul squirmed at first and wouldn't talk to us. We were happy about that, we didn't like what he might say.

The next Sunday after that, when we got out of the car, Joe came strolling across the grass. He was clean and dressed in a nice, white shirt and tie. He looked like he had been over to Aunt Ethel's for a haircut. I didn't want him for Aunt Ethel. Emma was for him even if she is real old. He didn't stink either.

Daddy shook his hand, patted him on the back, Mama smiled and said she was glad he was well, and it was nice to see him out. I thought it was nice he took a bath and combed his hair, but I didn't say so. I just said hello. He patted me on my ugly bonnet. Maybe Emma would be to church so she could see how nice he looked and want to be his mama. She needed someone too.

Mr. Sorenson and his wife Priscilla were standing by the door. I didn't look at him. The less eye contact, the better. He shook hands with Daddy and Mama. Lots of hellos were said, but not by me.

When he saw Joe, he laughed, said hello, and asked if Joe felt a little out of place at church. It was almost as if he didn't like Joe. Joe and Priscilla were gawking at each other, but when Mr. Sorenson said that, Joe shrank about two inches, turned red, and looked like he was going to bolt out of there, almost like a wild horse out of the chute.

Daddy put his hand on Joe's arm and guided him into the chapel. He looked at Mr. Sorenson and said Joe felt right at home in church. Mr. Sorenson let out another laugh. Mrs. Sorenson was awfully quiet, I don't think he lets her talk very much. She acted like she was ashamed of Mr. Sorenson's talk.

Joe was hurt. He never came to church after that, but he did continue to bathe so he didn't stink. Emma was sick that Sunday, so she didn't get to see Joe looking clean and handsome.

I wondered if Paul and Joe felt a little bit alike. Paul was always clean but didn't really have any friends. Sherry and I only play with him so he won't tattle on us. Joe has some friends, but most of them aren't clean. That night, I started to brush my hair, so I could get to be pretty.

A week or so later, when Beverly came home from school, she said that all the kids at school were called into the principal's office, one at a time. Clay Oliver and Mr. Sorenson interrogated them. Mama says that means to question them. There were only a couple of the big boys that didn't cry. Everyone else cried cause they thought they were going to jail for something they didn't do.

Mr. Sorenson was sure it was a student cause the writing and spelling was so bad. When Sherry heard that, she was really sad. She's real proud to know how to write. Clay thought the letter was a disguise, that some older person had it in for Mr. Sorenson.

Everyone in town was mad at Mr. Sorenson for questioning their kids like that. Clay went creeping around town in his horse-drawn buggy looking for a killer. He can't afford a car. He must have thought he was some big city sheriff, but he sure looked silly.

It's True, Honest!

Sherry and I went over to Paul's house everyday to see if he could play. We had to keep on his good side. Most of the time, he would tell his mama he didn't feel good and didn't want to play with us. This looked bad, because Paul was always happy to play with anybody that would play with him. When she started to ask him questions about us, he told her he didn't want to play with girls. I could see her mind working about the whole thing, so Sherry and I stopped going over there for a few days.

Instead, we walked down the lane towards Cleveland's pond. We could hear a lot a screaming and hollering coming from the pond. We crept through the underbrush and bushes to see what was happening.

We could see about five, big boys, almost as old as John, swimming and splashing in the water. They were "swimming in the raw." Their mamas would sure be upset if they found out.

Sherry was right. They did have extra parts! I was sure glad I'm a girl. I don't want those doodads.

We started to crawl back through the bushes. We didn't want to be seen.

It was about that time that we spotted their clothes scattered in piles on the ground. Sherry thought it would be funny to hide them. We hurried and gathered up every thing except their shoes, then made a mad dash toward the lane.

As we were running past some old, half-dead trees. Sherry was leading the way with me a couple of steps behind her. She tripped on a dead branch and fell flat on her face. It was a hard fall. Especially, when I stumbled too, landing up on top of her, and pushing her face down again. Her nose was bleeding hard and running onto one of the shirts. I cut my knee and it was bleeding too. We used one of the shirts to stop the blood and clean ourselves off.

About that time, we heard a commotion over by Smith's field just south of the railroad tracks. Leaving the clothes over in the grass under a tree, Sherry crept closer. I followed. Max Smith was arguing with a dirty man carrying a sack on his back. The man turned and came over close to where we were hiding. Max went back to the other side of the field.

The dirty man sure did stink, even worse than Joe. I was glad Joe had started bathing. I like Joe and wouldn't want him to look like a bum. Sherry said this man was a hobo and sometimes they kill little girls and eat them for dinner.

We didn't move an inch. Wide eyed, we watched as he picked up the clothes we had dropped. He threw the bloody shirt onto the ground and put all the other things into his sack, that is, all except a pair of pants. Then he quickly changed pants and ran over to the train tracks leaving his own tattered pants laying by the bloody shirt. Within ten minutes, he was hopping a freight train going west.

After seeing the tramp leave on the train, we went over to Granny P.'s and sat on her porch steps. About an hour later, five, sun-burned, sheepish-looking boys came sneaking into town, their front and back sides were covered with little branches of leaves.

The guys down at the Shell service station were the first to spot the shy little group. Of course, they laughed and yelled funny things at the boys and some of the town's people heard the commotion and came to witness the procession in the "raw." Johnny Dennison's mama who is really nervous and high-strung, was in the Red and White market. When she saw her darling, little Johnny walking up the street covered with only the green leaves of nature, she came unglued. Susan Benington helped her to a chair and gave her a cold cloth to help her shock.

Clay Oliver came on the scene and was going to arrest the boys for indecent exposure. They didn't expose anything. Their extra parts were all covered. I know, cause I peeked. He's always trying to put somebody in jail, but never has. I was really glad he wasn't to church the day I took a swim.

Elmer Brown told Clay someone had stolen all their clothes. Clay got into his buggy and hurried over to Cleveland's pond. All he could find was a bloody shirt and a pair of ragged pants. Max Smith said they belonged to a tramp he had seen earlier in the day. Clay said it looked like someone had done in the poor, ole cuss and he would catch the dirty rotten bum. Only, he used some of Joe's French, but it should be called Clay's French, since he uses it now and Joe don't. Granny P. told Sherry and I to come into the house, she didn't want us around that kind of talk.

Sherry and I continued to sit quietly on the steps, listening to everything. I didn't know if I should be worried that Clay would find out what happened to the clothes, or try out some of the words that other people in town used but weren't allowed in our family.

Clay told everyone to lock their doors and keep a close watch that night cause a killer was in town. Joe Peterson told Clay that, "there ain't been no killin cause there ain't no body."

I noticed Mr. Sorenson didn't say a word. His face looked like Joe's did when he was sick, all white.

Trial by fire

*A*t dinner, I asked Mama what a tramp is and if they killed and ate little girls. She smiled and said no, they didn't eat little children. Mama said that millions of men were out of work because of something called a depression, whatever that is. They were wandering around the country, hoping to find work. Many people referred to them as tramps or hobos. She said most of them were cold and hungry.

Charlotte wondered if the hobo had been killed. Daddy said he didn't think so. Clay should be smart enough to investigate before jumping to conclusions.

The next day, Sherry and I were playing in my sand pile when Paul came wandering over to play. He was really putting on an act; he usually walks straight. That day he acted like he wasn't sure of anything or even where to go.

The three of us started making tunnels in the sand, when all of a sudden, Paul stopped playing and asked us when we killed the dirty man. We said we never killed anybody. He looked really disappointed.

Sherry said we were nice girls and didn't kill people or animals. I said we only smashed spiders and dried worms in the sun. He said he didn't want to play anymore and started to leave, so Sherry said we liked him; I know that was a half a lie because we only like him some of the time. It made him happy though, he smiled and said he liked us too, but his mama wanted him to come home. Sherry left too.

After lunch, Beverly and I were finishing the dishes when a soft knock came at the front door. Beverly hurried to answer. That way I could be drying more of the dishes than she did. She worked out things like that.

It was Susan and her boy, Roger. He makes me nervous. I wanted to hide, so I stayed out of sight in the kitchen, although I listened to every word being said in the living room.

Mama kept asking Beverly where I was, but I was very quiet and stayed over in the corner. Finally, Mama came into the kitchen and found me. She said Roger had come with his mama and I should take him outside to play. I couldn't move. Those big, brown eyes just stared at me. They were the nicest eyes I had ever seen and me with little, short, stubby hair and green eyes. Oh, I couldn't say a word, I just stood there and he did too.

About that time, John came in from the field to fetch a bag of water. He said he would saddle ole Meg and we could ride down the lane. Roger had never been on a horse before, so he was excited. I was scared, cause we would need to ride double and that meant we would be touching each other.

We rode up and down the lane five times, me in front and him behind me with his arms around my tummy. He held tight so he wouldn't fall off. Soon we were laughing and having a good time. I know that he would rather have played with Sally Brown or Lucy Sorenson. They were pretty, but they sure weren't fun to play with. They play with dolls and don't ride horses or get dirty.

When he and Susan left to go home, he said he had a nice time and would like to come again. Susan smiled at me. Inside, I really didn't want him to come and play again cause I didn't like to feel sweaty, nervous and scared.

Two days later, Sherry and I were playing in the bushes where we had seen the tramp. There was a little shelter in the dried underbrush. It was covered over with branches. It was someone's hiding place. There were a few cans of food and some cigarettes in a dirty, cloth, flour sack. This was the home of a tramp. I quickly closed the sack and put it back in the weeds. Sherry kept the cigarettes. We ran over to Sherry's house and took some matches from the cupboard.

There was a nice, little place east of town. Sometimes, we would go there to play we were pioneers living in the wilderness. It was away from the farms and houses, with a cool stream nearby. This would be a good place to try smoking.

It wasn't fun like we thought it would be. All that smoke got drawn inside of us and made us cough, and besides, it made us stink. Now I know why some people carry that smell around with them. We kept trying, thinking it would get to be more fun, but it wasn't. It's a stupid habit.

Sherry started to looked green. She had thrown her cigarette over in the weeds next to mine. We were both sick. The little breeze helped, but not much. We were laying on our backs, wishing we had never seen cigarettes, when the smell of smoke and a cracking sound caught our attention.

We didn't know how to put out a fire, so we ran down the back road to Granny P.'s house and hid in her cellar. She saw us and knew something was wrong. Neither Sherry nor I would answer her questions. We didn't dare to tell her what we had been doing, but she sniffed a little and seemed to know anyway.

The big bell on the school house started ringing. They ring it to warn everyone when there is an emergency. This time it was a blazing fire east of town. Women were gathering in the street to watch the commotion. The men, grabbing shovels and rakes, ran to the fire station.

Clay Oliver was trying to pump up the right, front tire on the fire engine. It was out of gas too, but Joe came running from the service station with some gas to get the engine started. Ten minutes later they were chugging up the street to put out the "blazing inferno" as Granny P. called it.

We didn't get to watch the excitement after that, cause we were busy getting our bottoms spanked, then Granny made us have a good washing to get rid of the smell. She said we stank. I don't know if Sherry knew how a spanking felt, but this was the first serious job I'd had. Granny had a pretty good swing for a little, old lady. Both of our seater ends were bright red after she got through. I'm glad she didn't teach Mama about paddlings.

We also had a good scolding. She told us we shouldn't be taking boy's clothes while they're skinny-dipping, or trying to burn down the town. She must be the only one in town that knows it was us that took the boy's clothes. If anyone else had known, we would have been in serious trouble. She lectured to us about doing nice things for people instead of creating problems.

Lucille Evans came over to tell Granny that Clay said somebody had deliberately set the fire and was trying to burn down the whole town, but had only gotten about thirty acres of grass and brush. However, it had come real close to the Brown and Sorenson homes. He said it was probably the same bastard that had killed the tramp. She used the real word.

Lucille said Mr. Sorenson thinks it is the same person that threatened to kill him and was really trying to burn Sorenson's house down. Lucille was half right on that score. It was the same persons that wrote the note.

Granny just sat and listened to Lucille ramble on. She would nod her head every so often. Of course, Lucille had to shout so Granny could hear. Granny P. never let on that it was us that started the fire.

After Lucille left, Granny gave us each a cookie and a little be-good, reminder swat on our bottoms as we went out the door. She said she loved us and for us to please try to be good girls.

Sherry and I tried real hard to be helpful. We stayed home in the mornings, trying to make life easier for our mamas. Sherry tended her baby brother a lot. I helped pick peas and shell them so Mama could put them into bottles. Usually, in the afternoons we played in the sand pile. We didn't go too far from home.

Two days later, Mama made us each a peanut butter and honey sandwich. She said we could have a picnic in the orchard. She said we needed a break, but I think it was her that needed the break. I had been too much help.

We asked for some sacks like the tramps used. This was to carry our food and sweaters. Mama thought that was a cute idea. She gave each of us an old flour sack. We put our necessities in them, tied them on the end of two sticks, threw the sticks over our shoulders and headed out into the wilds of nature.

I told Sherry that the tramps would probably love a peanut butter sandwich. She thought so too. We put the remainder of our sandwiches back into our sacks and walked over near the railroad tracks where we had seen the hobo hideaway. No one was around, so we crept closer. We took the leftover part of our picnic lunches, still wrapped in the newspaper wrapping, and tucked them into a little cubbyhole under the bushes.

We ran back to where we could watch, but not be seen by a tramp when he came by. We laid in the bushes waiting for some kind of action. Nothing happened.

The afternoon freight train woke us both up. We had both fallen asleep. We weren't used to all the work we had been doing. The freight started to slow and two, dirty, ragged men jumped off. They seemed to be looking for some markings and finally ended up in the hobo hideout. Once, John had said that they have markings to tell each other where they can get food and help.

The two men ate our lunches in about two bites. They sure had poor manners. Maybe it was because they were so hungry. After they finished their sandwiches, they headed over into the thicket. We didn't see them after that.

Helping the Needy

Sherry and I had finally stumbled onto helping someone in need. We felt good, but we were sure hungry, cause we only had a tiny bite of lunch. We didn't bother to play anymore. We hurried home for something to eat.

At supper, Daddy said John would be taking a wagonload of supplies up to Grandpa Swensen at the sheep camp. Grandma Swensen was going with and would be staying with Grandpa for two weeks. Daddy asked me if I would like to go and help Granny Swensen take care of Grandpa.

It sounded like a great idea. I guess Mama was all helped out, now it was Grandma's turn.

The sheep camp was up in the hills and there really wasn't much for me to help with, except get dry wood for the camp-fire. Grandma cooked lots of mutton and sourdough bread. Grandpa took care of the sheep. Shep, the dog, helped him. I mostly played in the dirt, then Grandma would have me bathe in the "raw" over in the creek.

On my second dip, I forgot to put my clothes over in the bushes and they washed downstream. My other play dress was at home, in the dirty clothes to be washed. Granny would wash my dress out by hand every night, then it dried on the bushes while I slept. I was left with nothing but mother nature to cover me.

Grandma cut the sleeves out of an old shirt of Grandpa's and made me an ankle-length smock. We tied a string around my waist for a belt. It was nice and big, which gave me a wild and free feeling.

It was fun to play in the dirt and let the sun shine on me. I didn't wear my hat, so my hair could get plenty of sunshine and grow fast, but my skin started to get awfully dark. Grandpa said, if I had brown eyes, I could pass for an Indian girl. That made me real happy. I would love to be an Indian princess like "Minnie Hawchaw" in the funny papers. I wondered if it was possible to color my eyes.

One day, Clay Oliver came bounding into camp. He asked Grandpa where was Henry and Gwen Swensen's little girl. Grandpa pointed to where I was playing in the dirt. Clay said my clothes were found floating down the creek, and he was sure I had been drowned. Grandpa laughed and said I was too busy to let the water get me under.

———

Clay looked at me and said I didn't look like Henry's brat. This made Grandma mad, but she didn't say anything. Grandpa reassured him that I was Tillie Swensen. Clay said I was too dark and had a little bit of hair, it was like normal people. He said Henry's kid looked like some outer-space character from "Buck Rogers." This made me feel real bad.

Clay stayed for dinner. All the while, he kept looking at me like I was an imposter. We sure need a different town cop, a smarter one.

It was Leland that brought the next load of supplies. Grandma stayed with Grandpa and I went home with Leland.

After we pulled into the yard, Mama came running from the house, looked right past me and asked where I was. Then, it dawned on her that I was her little angel. She laughed and danced because I had enough hair to try and curl. She was happy to see me, but mostly my hair.

The next day was church. Mama curled my hair in the little, metal curlers. Since it was only about two inches long, the curls were real tight to my head. John said I looked like a pretty, little, mulatto girl, whatever that is. I told him I wanted to be a Indian princess.

I asked Mama if I could wear my ugly bonnet to church. She said no, I should show off my beautiful hair. I used some of the French words and said my hair was uglier than my bonnet. I also worked up a few tears for effect, but the effect was that the whole family closed in on me when I said those forbidden words that seemed to be spoken everywhere but in our family. Daddy said that when we say swear words, it shows we are lacking in good speech. He said it is nicer to hear good words. Emma is the only one in town with good speech.

At church, nobody sat by me, not even Sherry and Paul. They didn't even say hello. Roger, of course, was hemmed in by Sally Brown and Lucy Sorenson. He didn't even look at me. I thought that the next time he wants to ride Meg, he can walk for all I care.

There were two new boys in our class, twins. When our teacher said we had some new friends in our class, I looked at the twins. Paul and Sherry looked at me. When teacher asked me my name, I felt like giving her a left to the jaw, but instead, I meekly said Matillda Swensen. I didn't like the way everyone was looking at me. No one even seemed to recognize me. After the teacher asked my name, Sherry and Paul realized it was me. They were so happy to see me, they came and sat by me.

Paul wanted to know if an angel had painted my skin. I told him no, Heavenly Father was the one that changed my color and he had done it with lots of dirt and sun. Paul reached out to touch my arm. I could tell he was impressed. Sherry said she liked my hair and was it real?

The twins were named Burt and Bart Hussy and were dressed in fancy city suits. They were bigger than the rest of us in the class. With a name like Hussy, they would need to be bigger to hold their own. They turned out to be a little pushy with us smaller kids. After church, when we were outside, they pulled faces at me and said I was a funny-looking girl. Then, I heard Lucille Evans say their mama was divorced. That means that the daddy and mama are divided into two. Lucille also said that Mrs. Hussy was an old friend of Mr. Sorenson's. Even back then, I thought I could smell a rotten pot boiling.

Sherry and I spent all our spare time finding food and clothes for the tramps traveling through town.

Mama made bread on Monday morning. I helped Beverly

and Charlotte clean the house, then Mama told me I could play.

I grabbed my hat, put on my boots and quickly stuffed a fresh loaf of bread into my hobo sack. Of course, this was when Mama wasn't looking.

Sherry and I gathered some ripe apples from the orchard. As we were passing Mabel Stewart's house, we noticed she was cooling two cherry pies on her windowsill. There were only four in their family, so one pie was plenty for them. It was good we each had a hobo sack because they were getting pretty full.

Joe Peterson's long handle underwear was hanging on the clothesline. A tramp was more in need of them than Joe. Joe had a warm house on cold nights.

On the way to the hobo hut, we passed Burt and Bart Hussy's house. Their mother was walking down the street toward town. I never in my life saw anyone like her. First of all, she smelled just like a flower garden without the manure. Sherry said the smell was from perfume. The rich, city women wear it a lot, perfume,…not manure. Her upper part had a furry thing wrapped around. I guess she didn't have a coat. Poor thing! Maybe her daddy had to kill their dog and use the skin to keep her warm. Sherry told me that rich, city women also wear furs. Her hair was colored bright red. I wanted to ask if she could color eyes brown, but I didn't dare to speak. She smiled and said hello and clicked right on down the rocky road in her high-heeled shoes. She was having a hard time walking.

We passed Granny P.'s house, she waved to us from the swing on her front porch. She gave us a "be good girls" look.

After crossing the railroad tracks, we waited until there was no one in sight, then put the food and long handles in the tramp hut. After that, we beat it for home as fast as our legs would go.

We were both hungry 'cause we had saved our lunch sandwiches for the tramps. Sherry stopped at her house, cause she wanted to listen to "Little Orphan Annie" before supper. I went on home.

When I reached the creek by our farm yard, I could see Susan Benington's car parked by our gate. I wondered if brown-eyed Roger was with her. I was in no mood to sweat and get nervous, so I hid over in the bushes by the creek. I laid there until it was time for Leland and I to fetch the cows from the pasture.

I walked over to the house to wait for Leland. Susan and Roger were just leaving. He said he was sorry we didn't get to play. I thought, you're sorry you couldn't play with Sally Brown and Lucy Sorenson. He makes me feel weird every time I look at him. I don't like that, but he is nice to look at if he doesn't know I'm peeking.

At supper, Mama said that she and Susan would be making cookies for the Halloween party at school. She asked if I would like to help. I asked if Roger was going to help. She said maybe. I told her that I would think about it.

I asked Mama and Charolette if they could make me into a pretty girl. Mama laughed and gave me a squeeze. She said I was one of the prettiest girls she had ever seen. That's the only lie I have ever heard Mama tell. Maybe she needs some of those eyeglasses like Grandpa uses to read with.

Mama is pretty and she has nice manners. I wouldn't mind growing into a nice, pretty lady like her, but I would want to take my time and not grow too fast. I like the way I am now, but someday it would be okay.

Charolette thinks pretty hair makes a difference. She brushes her hair a hundred strokes every night and morning. I started to brush mine a hundred strokes that very night, but I did worry about wearing it out and being bald again. Mama told me not to worry, my hair would grow faster and have a nice shine if I brushed it like Charolette brushes her's.

A Theft at the Bank

Sherry and I worked real hard the next few days. Rearranging the extras in town was a lot of work, but the tramps passing through town needed food and warm clothing if they were going to survive the cold weather.

One day when I went with Mama into the bank, I saw Mr. Brough, the bank man, counting a bunch of paper money. He's our mayor too. It was in a lot of different piles. My word, he didn't need all those dollars. I didn't know he was that selfish. He and Mama went over to set down at a desk. I followed, but first I put one of the piles in my hat and quickly put my hat back on my head. Ruth Tinney came over to finish the counting job for Mr. Brough.

Before we left to go over to the Red and White Market, some of the bank people seemed to be a little excited about something. Then, Clay Oliver came rushing in.

He started asking questions and poking his nose into bank business. Mama said that there had been a theft, whatever that means. She said there was one hundred dollars missing. Now I know what theft means.

Sherry and I put the money into a little wooden cigar box in the underbrush where we hid when we spied on the tramps. Each day, when we put food and clothes out for the tramps, we put a a piece of the paper money with it. Sherry said the piece was a five-dollar bill, she knows her numbers.

When I went home, Susan and Roger were there to make

cookies. I started to sweat as usual. I don't know why Roger makes me feel so icky. Even my heart goes fast when he's around.

We played in the cookie dough and helped frost them, then it was time to fetch the cows. Roger helped me. I was beginning to think he liked to play with me.

Roger said he was going to be a cowboy for Halloween. I wanted to be a tramp. When I told Mama that I couldn't bathe or wash until after Halloween, so I could stink real good, she tried to talk me into being a princess. I bawled and refused, but Mama won the round on the washing and bathing bit.

Sherry and I both dressed as tramps. We put on ragged clothes and carried our hobo sticks.

On the way to the school house, we stopped at the creek and daubed mud on our faces. If we were going to be hobos, we needed real, live dirt.

At the school, we went in the big, double doors. Everyone was in the gym playing games and going through the spook alley, that is everyone except Bobbie Stewart and Michael Evans. They had been doing some mischief in Mr. Sorenson's office. We waited until they joined the party in the gym, then we went in to see what they had been up to. At first, everything looked normal, then we noticed a hangman's noose hanging over Mr. Sorenson's chair. Good job! We thought we would add to it, so we got busy picking our noses. We needed lots of blood. It took a few minutes to get a nice puddle. We dipped our fingers in the runny, red stuff. Sherry wrote U R DED again, just like she did the other time, and I drew a picture of a man with a noose around his neck. I made the picture with some of the blood.

When we finished, we went into the gym and played some of the games. Roger was playing with Lucy and Sally. He looked like a handsome cowboy and never even looked at me. I felt ugly. That was when I told Sherry I wanted to go home. I told Mama we were through Halloweening and were going home. She said to go straight home.

On the way past the kitchen, we noticed no one was tending the goodie table, so I scooped all the cookies into Sherry's tramp sack and continued on to the big, double doors. Mr. Sorenson's new, winter jacket was hanging by his office. He had a nice job and could get another one. The poor tramps of this world couldn't even get work. I put the coat into my sack.

We hadn't seen Mr. Sorenson at the party, but decided he must be somewhere in the building.

Sherry thought it would be best to take our loot over to the hideout in the under brush before we went home.

When we passed the Hussy house, there were two people standing on the front porch. One looked like Mr. Sorenson. We ran over behind a tree to get a better look. Bess Hussy and Mr. Sorenson were standing there kissing each other. It was so dark, we had to look real hard. My mama and daddy kiss, but he don't kiss other women. All of a sudden, I felt sorry for Lucy.

We didn't dare to move. Mr. Sorenson's jacket was in my sack and we couldn't let him see us. We just watched them. They sure acted weird.

Sherry and I were both in shock. Her eyes were big like half-dollars. She said mine were too. She didn't know anymore of why they were acting so stupid than I did.

After Mr. Sorenson left, we ran as fast as we could to the hideout in the underbrush, hid the jacket and cookies, then both headed for home at top speed. As we passed Granny P.'s house, I thought I saw her watching us from her upstairs window.

When we came to Sherry's lane, I left her and started to run for home, and I could hear some giggling from two Halloweeners up ahead of me. They just stood there in their costumes, waiting until I got to where they were standing. I was nervous, but thought I shouldn't show it.

It was Burt and Bart. Burt was dressed like a skeleton and Bart like the devil with a little pitch fork. They started to laugh and make fun of me, then Burt pushed me down and Bart snatched my sack to see if I had any goodies. While they were looking in my sack, I pushed Burt down and stood on him with my feet. I could see that the way Leland taught me to box wouldn't work in this situation, this was a street-brawl. Bart came at me with his fork and hit me in the face. He cut my cheek. Burt grabbed my feet and made me lose my balance and I fell on my back, then Burt sat on my tummy and began pounding me in the face with his fists, while Bart beat me with my hobo stick.

I didn't cry cause they would think they were winning, so I shouted that I was gonna tell Clay Oliver on them and he would arrest them and put them in jail. They just laughed at me and kept on beating my face, so I yelled as loud as I could that I was gonna tell the whole town on their mama and Mr. Sorenson. They stopped beating me, dropped my stick and ran away. I wouldn't really tell on their mama and Mr. Sorenson, cause it would hurt Lucy and Priscilla Sorenson.

I got up off the ground and cried all the way home. Mama and Daddy were both really upset when they saw me, but I told them I just fell down. I know they knew I was fibbing cause they said everything would be okay and I wouldn't get into trouble if I told them who had done it, but I didn't dare.

John and Leland both said I had a beautiful shiner and looked like I had been through the big war. Charolette and Beverly said it was because I was dressed like a hobo instead of a princess. Mama was all fired up about the whole thing and I could see the wheels turning in Daddy's head. I think he was planning to get to the bottom of it all.

———

The next day was Friday. I was helping Mama clean up the breakfast, cause the older kids were at school. Mama kept talking about the night before, hoping I would open up and tell who had beaten me up. She was really making me nervous, so nervous that I dropped a bottle of milk.

She didn't scold me, she just said to clean it up. I said I wanted to go over to Sherry's house first and then I would. She said no, it would be sour and stink if I waited, so I said she could clean it up. She said that when we make a mess, it is important to clean things up and the sooner it is done, the easier it is to do. I bawled, half cause I had to clean up the milk and half cause I still hurt from my beating.

Mama said she would help me and would always help me when I needed help. I think she was really giving me one of her lectures. That made me feel lots better. That is, until later in the day.

Paul was having his Friday afternoon fling in my sand pile. Both he and Sherry kept asking about the black marks on my eye and face. Paul wanted to know if the angel was upset with me and had put them there. I couldn't tell them what happened, cause Lucille would find out and tell the whole town.

Before long, Paul's big brother, Michael came over to fetch him home. Michael said there had been a lot of commotion at school. Somebody had threatened to kill Mr. Sorenson, just like the other time. He said they had found a lot of bloody writing saying they were going to hang Mr. Sorenson. He didn't let on that it was he and Bobbie who put the noose above Mr. Sorenson's chair. He just rambled on about the blood. He said there was going to be a town emergency meeting to discuss all the crime in town and Lucille wanted Paul at home.

I asked what was crime and Sherry said grime was a lot of dirt. Michael said no, this was crime, breaking the law, like stealing, killing and things like that.

Well, Sherry and I were both surprised. We didn't know about things like that. Sherry asked what was stealing. Michael said it was taking things that belong to someone else and Clay was going to catch the dirty, then he copy-catted Clay with some of the French words. Daddy was right, swearing does send out a signal that we are lacking in good speech. Michael sounded dumb. But, when he said that Clay was gonna put whoever it was in jail, it didn't sound dumb, it sounded scary.

Sherry was frightened and wanted to go home. I was scared too. The sand pile wasn't fun any more.

At dinner, Daddy said that Joe Peterson told Clay that Mr. Sorenson didn't get a death threat, it was just kids playing Halloween tricks and were getting back at him cause he's been so mean to them.

Mama said Joe and Mr. Sorenson had been bitter enemies ever since Mr. Sorenson moved to town and wooed Priscilla Sorenson away from Joe, and that Priscilla must regret not choosing Joe. It had broken both their hearts.

Daddy said something about little ears listening and started saying he wished he could get enough money together to build a bedroom. Maybe he could get some of his lambs to market this year.

John and Leland had been sleeping on the far end of the back porch ever since they were little. It was pretty nice except in the winter time. During the real cold weather, Mama heated rocks in the oven and put in their beds to help keep the boys warm.

Sometimes, the snow would blow through the cracks in the wood, but they had a canvas tarp covering their bed to keep dry.

Our house only has three rooms plus the back porch and pantry. Us girls sleep in the living room on the fold-down couch.

It would be nice to have a real bedroom for my brothers. I thought how nice it would be for the tramps to have a warm room and good food. Even though I felt happy for John and Leland if Daddy were able to sell some lambs, I felt sick inside about my future.

The big school bell began ringing to tell everyone it was time for the crime meeting. Daddy and Mama put on their coats and left. Charolette, Beverly and I washed up the dishes. As soon as we had the kitchen cleaned, I went to bed without brushing my hair. I wouldn't be needing long, beautiful hair where I was going. I wondered if Roger would ever play with me again.

On Saturday morning, Sherry and I were talking about whether or not to get something for the tramps. I said we had been stealing. Sherry said it wasn't stealing if you gave it to other people. That sounded right but we wanted to make sure. In the meantime, we better fetch Mr. Sorenson's jacket, the cookies and the money, and return them to their proper places.

When we reached our hiding place, everything was gone, the coat, food and money, all gone! Nothing was left except the smashed grass and bushes.

On the way back home, we could see a woman over in the trees. Sherry said it looked like someone was cutting a spanking willow. I looked more closely. It was Granny P! Sherry recognized her at the same time I did.

We both threw down our hobo sacks, covered our

bottoms with our hands and ran faster than our legs had ever moved before.

Up the sidewalk towards home we ran, tears and screams coming from our upper parts, our hands still covering our lower parts and Granny coming behind at a good steady pace.

When we reached the corner, we turned up Main Street. There were several people that came out of their houses to check on the tears. We didn't answer their questions. We kept moving as fast as we could. At the Red and White market, customers interrupted their shopping to step outside and watch the circus. I saw Roger out of the corner of my eye. He was peeking through the big glass window. Of course, the men at the Shell service station were already on hand to watch all the happenings in town. The goings on in town is their only entertainment.

Granny was losing ground, but kept coming, tapping the willow against the ground with every step.

When we came to Evan's road, Sherry parted company and headed for home. She didn't even say good-bye. I just kept running and screaming until I reached the creek. Then I thought I had better cut the noise.

Granny P. Worries

Matilda Patterson sat at the window in her darkened upstairs bedroom. Her eyes alert, she scanned the night, watching for any movement of costumed, young people reveling in Halloween activities. She was always amazed at some of the pranks that were pulled on these October thirty-first nights.

Last year, Elmer Brown, Johnny Dennison and that group of boys had taken Lucille Evans' outhouse, uprooted it from the foundation and put it on the roof of their barn. Then, to add insult to misery, they hung a pair of George Evans' long handle underwear and a pair of Lucille's bloomers on the door for the whole town to view at sunrise the next morning.

Lucille should have known better than to leave her wash on the clothes line on Halloween night.

Matilda worried that some of the pranksters might zero in on her territory. So far, they had been very respectful of her being alone and advanced in years, but one never knows.

A sudden movement caught her eyes. She strained earnestly to make out the figure. No, there were two, smaller and much younger than Dennison and his friends. Oh, they seemed to be starting much younger these days. What was the world coming to?

The two, disguised images passed her house and headed toward the thicket over on the other side of the railroad tracks. Each was carrying hobo sacks and dressed as if they were some of those riding the rails.

Matilda's mind raced to her youngest granddaughter, Tillie and her friend. What was the other girl's name? Oh yes! Sherry, Sherry Allen, yes, yes, the new family living over on the old Holt farm.

She left her thoughts dangling as alarm rushed to her mind and an encroaching chill gripped her body. That was a dangerous area for two little girls to be venturing into, especially after dark. She had seen some pretty weird happenings over near those trees. Just earlier today, she had watched two filthy transients beat a woman. A few minutes later, all three sat on a rock, passed a bottle around, then vanished into the thick foliage.

When the freights came through, she always took time to scan the vicinity and be aware of any tramps in the area. She was wary of those wandering the countryside. They made her nervous. Clay Oliver may have his down side, but he did keep the vagabonds out of town.

Common sense told her she couldn't let two little girls go into those woods alone. As she grabbed her shawl from the hook, she continued to browse the dark shadows. Again there was movement. Emerging like two miniature phantoms, the childish figures came into view. The one on the left glanced up at her window. Yes, it was Tillie and her friend. The girls continued up the street toward home.

Matilda felt a temporary relief, but tomorrow, she would talk to Gwen. Surely, Gwen must have some idea of the child's wanderings. It was true, the child was strong-willed and adventurous, nevertheless, there should be tighter reins put on a little girl her age. Gwen was an exceptional mother, but Tillie was a real challenge to her and would be for any mother. Maybe it would be best to take care of the situation herself and not upset her daughter. Gwen certainly had her hands full taking care of her family, why add extra worries?

The frail, little woman returned her shawl to the hook on the closet door and prepared for bed. Warm quilts and soft bedding brought little relief to the old woman's body, and sleep refused to settle in. Her mind rested on the two girls and dwelled there until wee hours, even then, rest had abandoned her weary soul.

Friday morning, the town was awakened to witness the changes made by the Halloweening youngsters. Three of Max Smith's cows were tied to the door knob of the Red and White

Market. Mr. Brown's pregnant cats were all put in a grain sack and delivered to Emma's door step. Stewart's picket fence was torn down and put around Lucille Evans' calf pen, Mr. Sorenson's outhouse was put out in the street in front of his home and a good many windows were decorated with soap writings. Of course, the less serious antics were not as high on the list of conversational topics.

After lunch, Matilda began washing her dishes, when a knock came to her front door. She could see Henry's mother, Faye Swensen, through the glass window. Turning the key, she opened the door.

"Hello Faye, come in." She stepped aside, holding the door.

"How are you Matilda?" Faye shouted, so the deaf woman could hear. "I thought I'd just drop by and see if you are okay. Why did you have your door locked? Have you been having trouble?"

Matilda, cupping her left ear with her hand, answered, "Yes, yes, I'm fine. I just haven't been out yet this morning. How are you, Faye?"

Matilda, her voice softer than usual, sounded unconvincing and preoccupied. Faye sensed this.

"Are you sure? I just felt like I should stop by. Did you have trouble with the young people last night?"

"Heavens no. They never bother me. I guess they think I'm too old to put up with it. But, they always give Max Smith a hard time and he's the same age as me."

"That's because he's a grouch. That farm's getting too much for him. He needs help with it. I think the kids work all year at new ideas to get even with him and Horace Sorenson." She paused, then went on. "I understand there was another threatening note left in Mr. Sorenson's office last night."

Matilda made no reply. Her hand still cupped to her ear, she waited patiently for the younger woman to continue.

"The first time, someone put a dead rattlesnake on his desk. This time, they had a hangman's noose. Both times, there was lots of blood and a note saying he was dead. Doesn't that sound like kids to you?" Faye didn't wait for Matilda to answer. "I think it's only natural the kids would try to upset him. He's always thought he was a little above the rest of us. No wonder no one likes him." Faye rested her tirade.

Matilda's only response was, "Poor Priscilla."

"Are you sure everything's alright? You look tired. Need anything from the store? I can pick it up for you."

"No, no. I'm fine. I think I'll just rest a bit."

After Faye left, Matilda went upstairs to rest. Still exhausted from the previous night, sleep almost immediately overtook the frail, thin body.

Little Tillie soon made a visit to her Granny's dreams. The picture of a wee babe wrapped in flannel and placed in a cardboard box, warming on the oven door, became vivid as the woman slumbered. She could feel the soft warmth as the first cries burst from the tiny lungs. Other past images of her precious, little grand-daughter unfolded while she slept away the afternoon. Love, mingled with concern, having engulfed her soul, made her sleep restless. Then peace descended upon her and she slept on into the night. She did not awake until dawn.

Still troubled and uncertain as to what action should be taken to help Tillie, Matilda pondered the matter all Saturday morning as she went about her household chores. She was so absorbed in her thoughts of Tillie, she was unaware that she had failed to polish her lamp table and left the swept-up pile of dirt by the dust bin. She had merely gone through the actions of her labor, while her mind wrestled with her granddaughter.

About midmorning, she glanced out the kitchen window in time to see the tail end of the two little imps, toting two hobo sacks fastened to sticks, disappear into the trees. The one in the print dress and light sweater had a man's western hat riding her ears. She wore over-sized, cowboy boots.

Strong measures must be taken. Matilda stood motionless, watching the girls, then quickly moved into action. Without stopping for a wrap or shawl, she went out the back door and headed for a stand of willows. She had broken off one with a good spring and turned just in time to see the two girls emerge from the thicket.

Seeing her with the willow, the girls immediately threw down their sticks, covered their bottoms with their hands, burst into tears and started to run. Both were aware they had ventured into forbidden territory and each had a vivid memory of the last time Granny had paddled their bottoms.

Matilda treaded through the wild grass, stopped long enough to pick up the girl's hobo sticks and sacks, then fell in behind them. She couldn't help but smile to herself as she watched the girls running up the street, screaming at the top of their lungs. Some of her own misdeeds of early childhood pierced her memory. That recall seemed to soften her heart a bit and bring to light a better understanding of the innocence of the girls. Tillie still needed some new direction, but with a softer touch.

She continued to follow at a good pace for her age, but was losing ground. The sight of the old hat bouncing up and down on Tillie's head brought another smile. Maybe, she would just talk to Gwen and Tillie together.

On up Main Street, she followed the girls, her eyes straight ahead, her unhearing ears masking the chuckling comments from those witnessing the scene. Oh, she knew there would be a few words exchanged about the whole affair. She didn't care. She was far more concerned with Tillie's actions.

As she entered the Swensen yard, her breathing was rapid. It had been a brisk walk, much more than she was used to. She had lost sight of both of the girls several minutes before they entered the lane. They were surely anxious to put a good distance between themselves and her willow, but she had maintained her quick pace and was ready to face the little chits.

Gwen, seeing Matilda through the kitchen window, left her dishes and went outside to meet her mother.

"Mother, are you alright?" Concerned at the old woman's heavy breathing, then seeing the two hobo sticks, she asked, "What's wrong? Where's Tillie? Has something happened to her?"

Her loud words were received by the deaf ears. All that Matilda could say was, "Gwen—we need—to talk—about —Tillie." The old woman gasped between words. "She—and her—little friend—have—I need to sit a—minute."

Henry was emerging from the tool shed and seeing Matilda gasping for air, he immediately knew something must be amiss. With long, quick strides he soon joined the two women.

A few minutes later, Granny gave her daughter and son-in-law an account of what she knew of Sherry and Tillie's activities, and a summation of other possible wrongdoings, at which she was only guessing.

Henry and Gwen were both horrified at the possibility of their darling angel and Sherry being behind all the thefts in town. Gwen's mind raced to the day she and Tillie were in the bank and the unusual disappearance of the bills. Was it possible? No! She pushed the appalling thought from her mind of reality. Tillie would never do such a thing and if so, why? The idea brought a heavy, sick ache inside. Suddenly, she felt weak and tired. This was just too much.

She collected herself and they began calling for the little girl, but there was no answer. A few minutes later, John and Leland, then Charolette and Beverly joined in the hunt for their sister. Still, there was no answer.

Henry said, "She must have gone over to Sherry's. I'm going over and get her. I'll be back shortly."

In their race for home, Sherry had been a few steps in front of Tillie. Tears clouded her vision, masking the rocky road with a hazy covering. She stumbled on an unseen rock, catching her balance, she forged ahead. At the fork of the road, Sherry left her partner in crime without a word of farewell and dashed toward the tall weeds edging the granary in the Allen's barnyard.

Like Jesse James and other infamous criminals before her, she sought the refuge and protection of a hideout. Crouching low to the ground, her back against the studded, wood building, she kept her eyes peeled to the road, watching. There was no sign of Granny P. or Clay Oliver, the town sheriff.

The only one in sight was Henry Swensen. She decided that he must know of her deeds and realizing her future was in peril if she were found, she ran to a more substantial protection, a building with a lock on the door. A moment later, she was holed up inside the privy, with the door bolted.

She peered between the slats on the wooden door. Her father and mother were standing on the porch, talking to Henry. Then, her parents proceeded to call her. She didn't answer. They continued their summons. Still, no reply. Rusty, the family dog, anxious to serve his master, barked several times, then ran to the outhouse and commenced scratching and clawing at the door.

Sherry emerged. Unmistakable fear flew to her eyes as she faced her soon to be interrogator.

Sherry's parents stood silent, while Henry questioned Sherry about the girls' activities the past several months. Again, tears erupted as she made a detailed confession. She, like Tillie, also feared the possibility of going to that terrible place referred to as jail. Both girls knew it was a scary place, almost as bad as where the evil one called the devil is said to live.

Henry, along with Sherry's parents, were dumbstruck with the revelation as Sherry related her story. They were shocked at what had been going on right under their noses, and they had failed to see the misdeeds of the two, little girls.

Through sobbing tears, Sherry tried to explain that neither she nor Tillie realized they were stealing and they both were terribly sorry for what they had done. They had merely wanted to help the poor, hungry tramps.

The three adults listened tentatively, each silently questioning their own consciences for not being more aware of the girls' behavior. Ironically, each came to the same conclusion; each had neglected a particular segment of teaching honesty to their child, and each had isolated themselves from making an effort to give aid to those unfortunate men roaming the country.

The girls had seen a need, and in their own way, had tried to ease the plight of the ragged, hungry men.

Henry interrupted the thoughtful silence that hung in their midst. "We better get together with the girls and pay for the things they took." He paused, turned and looked toward home. "Right now, I'm going home and have a good talk with Tillie."

When Henry reached home, Tillie was not there.

The Town Unites

The warmth of the noon day sun felt good on his back. However, dark storm clouds could be seen in the far west. This was his favorite time of the year, chilly nights and brisk days. Clay Oliver basked in comfort as he steered his buggy toward the Stewart place. No need to rush. Everything was quiet and peaceful in town. Early yesterday morning, he had Dennison and his friends scrub the sidewalk in front of the Red and White market. Cows always leave a trail as well as a smell. Now he needed to check on Mabel's picket fence.

Joe Peterson was there supervising a half-dozen boys while they rebuilt it. Funny how boys could tear down a fence, cart it across town and reassemble it in an hour, but under supervision, take several days to restore it to it's original condition. Joe would make sure they did a good job. He liked the feeling of being in command. The only time he really experienced that bit of authority was the few days after Halloween, when the kids needed an overseer to make sure everything was put back in order.

———

The hard part of the whole situation was the money. The boys also had to purchase any broken boards. They had very little, if any, money.

The buggy came to a halt. Clay pushed his hat back on his head. "How's it goin' Joe?" Hammering in the background rang in competition with his words.

"Fine!" Joe turned to look at the boys nailing pickets to the top rail of the fence, then continued. "It took a while to get these kids goin', but their doing okay now. They're a learnin'. Get ol' Sorenson's toilet back in place?"

Clay was conscious that for the last six months, Joe's speech had been lacking in those descriptive words that had been his trademark in the past.

"Yep! Johnny and Elmer put it back yesterday. Too bad ol' Horace wasn't inside when they moved it the other night." Clay inserted a few colorful words, trying to impress Joe. "Better yet, they should've waited until he was inside and then just tipped it over and left. It'd serve him right to be trapped in the outhouse out in the street and nobody know where he's at." Again, some of the forbidden language was added.

Both men chuckled at the thought.

"What did ya think of the meeting last night?" inquired Clay.

"Thought it went good, but nothin solved. Things just don't make sense. Mostly, food and a few clothes are missin', but the money from the bank disappearin' into thin air, the fire east of town may not be connected…" Joe left his thoughts dangling, and noticing a boxelder bug on the ground, spit a spray of tobacco juice at the insect. The brown juice spewed a good six feet making a direct hit on the bug. Both men looked at the little, brown spot, Joe, proud of the long shot he'd made with the juice, let his eyes remain glued to the dampened target. Clay, on the other hand, was glad he didn't have that particular habit.

"What do ya think of ol' Horace's life threats? Do ya think it's kids?"

"Yep, and I don't think it's any tramps doin' the other stuff. They don't come over here, I make sure they don't come this side of the tracks. Anyway, they're usually only here a few hours or a day."

"Yeah, that's right."

Their attention was diverted by a commotion down the street. The screams carried through the block, as if a cannon had burst forth it's load in the quiet country air.

"Looks like Matilda's got her ire up," said Joe.

"Who wouldn't with that little Tillie? She's a handful. She sure ain't like her Ma."

"No, she ain't. Gwen's a real lady, refined and all. Always

has been, a beauty too. Tillie, on the other hand, ain't cut from the same beauty mold." Then, remembering Tillie's sudden appearance with her "magic get well box" and house cleaning job when he was sick, Joe added, "She's thoughtful like her Ma though. She does have that beautiful, olive skin. Maybe the looks `ll come later."

A silence began to open between them. Each man became immersed in his own thoughts. Ironically, their musing was very similar, each was acutely aware of his own uneasiness when Gwen was near. Yet, after a few minutes in her presence, her thoughtful, quiet manner helped restore their confidence and self-worth. From there, Joe's thoughts traveled to the similarity between Gwen and Priscilla Sorenson. An empty pang entered his stomach, then a sad cloud covered his eyes. Oh, for what might have been. Maybe, if he had worked on a little refinement, things would have been different.

Clay's voice brought him back to the present. "She seems to bring the best out in people; a good woman." The hammering ceased, and the boys began a little horseplay while they waited for further instructions.

A moment later, Clay flipped the reins, prodding the horse into movement and tipped his hat. "I better get goin', need to check on a few things."

"Yeah, me too," said Joe, turning in the direction of the boys and the half-finished fence.

A little later in the afternoon, Clay was driving past the creek and noticed a hat wedged among the protruding rocks. It was moored on the edge away from the rushing waters.

Stepping down from the buggy, he waded into the water and retrieved the headgear, then looked around. Nothing seemed to be amiss. He returned to his conveyance, climbed aboard and placed the sodden hat on the seat beside him.

For the next half-hour, Clay drove up and down the flowing water and close proximity. He watched the murky water make it's way, rushing unhindered between the steep banks. There were no visible prints in the mud, however, the tall grass edging the water was trampled in places. This was normal, since almost everyday, someone would fish the stream, hoping for a catfish.

He stood looking for any signs of the little girl, but the creek refused to yield any hidden secrets that might be lying within it's depths. Remembering Tillie's clothes floating down from the mountain sheep-camp, Clay surmised the little tyke had merely lost her hat in the mad dash for home. His mood was pensive as he walked back to his buggy. Nothing more unusual had attracted his attention.

He turned and proceeded down Main Street. Several minutes later, Lucille Evans ran out of the Red and White market and called to him.

"Clay! Clay!" she shouted, waving her arms above her head. "Clay! Little Tillie Swensen is missing. The family has been looking for her since just after noon." Then, seeing the wet hat on the seat beside Clay, her voice trembled, tears erupted and coursed down her cheeks.

She began to sob. "Harold and Susan are closing the store to go over and help."

"Thanks!" He began turning his buggy around, while Lucille continued to alert the town that Tillie was missing and now added that it looked as if she had drowned.

When Clay arrived at the Swenson place, there were several cars and a couple of buggies parked in the yard. Every foot of ground seemed to be covered by searching family and neighbors.

Clay looked around for Henry, then spotted him walking slowly along an irrigation ditch, probing it's depth and rummaging through the vegetation alongside the bank. Clay approached him. Henry had the saddest look that Clay had ever seen.

"Henry, did she ever reach home?"

"No. We've looked everywhere. I'm at my wit's end. I just can't believe it."

Hesitating briefly and unsure of himself, Clay said, "I found her hat floating in the creek about forty minutes ago. I've looked all up and down the banks, but couldn't find anything out of whack. It'll be dark in another hour. I'll arrange to get some lanterns and torches for the men. That seems to be the only logical place to look." Clay's dialogue lacked his usual adjectives. For some reason, he felt they would show disrespect for Tillie and her family. "Maybe, you better tell Gwen about the hat before Lucille gets to her."

Clay's words hit Henry like a ton of brick. The color swept from his face leaving a stark whiteness, a deathly, colorless image. He stood there, making every effort to hold himself together. He must, for Gwen's sake. He took a deep breath.

"You talk to her little friend, the Allen girl?"

"Yes." Henry's words were shaky. "Yes, I think those two little girls are the answer to a lot of the mischief that's been going on in town. When we couldn't find Tillie, I went over to the Allen place to fetch her home. Sherry said they parted at the head of the lane." His voice cracked. He waited a few seconds before continuing. "I had a good talk with her and her parents. She owned up that it was she and Tillie that have been the culprits in the thefts in town. They've been stealing in order to help the hobos passing through."

Henry wanted to get everything in the open. Clay had remained quiet. His face reflected his unspoken question. The answer came when Henry spoke again. "I talked to Brough, he's over in the orchard, looking; I'll go in to the bank on Monday and sign a loan for the money part. He'll accept my farm for collateral. I'm not going to concern myself with that right now. I've got to find Tillie first, then I'll take care of all the other."

The events of the past several months replayed in Clay's mind. He gathered his thoughts, then remarked, "If it weren't for the seriousness of Tillie missing, it would almost be a joke on all of us adults that those girls carried all that off right under our noses and none of us were the wiser. Right now, we better do the important thing; find Tillie."

A cluster of people were over near the orchard and trees beyond, calling Tillie's name and foraging through the bushes. Clay joined them, while Henry walked over to Gwen who was on the lawn with Susan.

"Honey," he said, his voice breaking. "Clay found her hat

floating in the creek. He's getting some lanterns and torches together for the men. We're going to concentrate the search," he said, nodding toward the creek, "over in that area."

He took Gwen into his arms and holding her tight, they both let their tears go. She shook uncontrollably; her tears soaked the front of his shirt. The autumn breeze brought a deep coldness where the tears rested on his chest; an unseasonal chill had invaded the area, almost as if snow were in the air. It was a draining effort to remain calm and strong. They stood embraced together, each trying to give strength and absorb it from the other.

Gwen's trembling stopped. She quietly whispered, "Dear Lord, please protect Tillie from further harm, and if she's passed from this life, please take good care of her and give us the strength to accept thy will. Please help us find her." She hesitated, then repeated the word, "please."

It was a simple prayer. After she had finished speaking, still holding her, Henry quietly added, "Yes, please dear Lord."

Finally, he said, "I better go help Clay."

She turned to Susan, and the crying started again. Each woman was keenly aware of the invisible cord forever tying a mother to her off-spring. The friends shared their tears while Roger, not quite understanding, clung to his mother's skirt.

Several minutes later, unknowingly, Gwen expressed the same thoughts her husband had minutes earlier, when she said, "I can't go to pieces now, not now. We have to keep looking." Glancing toward the house, she spoke to her friend. "Susan, I'm worried about Mother, she feels like it's all her fault. Can you talk to her? I've tried. Maybe she'll feel better if you tell her that she is in no way to blame."

The two women slowly walked to the porch where Matilda, her strength spent, rested in a rocking chair.

"Mother, come in the house and rest. You'll catch cold out here."

"No, I want to stay out here. I can keep watch from the porch. Inside, all I can see are the four walls."

Susan knelt beside the chair and began talking to the old

woman, while Gwen went into the kitchen and warmed a glass of milk for her mother. The women's voices carried through the screened door into the kitchen. Matilda's was low and trembling. Susan's, though loud for the deaf ears of this kind, wise woman, carried an understanding tone.

Gwen returned to the porch with the milk and a light coverlet. "Here, Mother, drink this. It'll give you a little strength and help your nerves." Unfolding the quilt, she carefully covered her mother, leaned over and kissed her forehead. Then, she said, "You stay here and rest for a while. Susan and I are going over to the creek and help look there."

The dark autumn night rang with the calling of "Tillie, where are you?" Torches and lanterns were held high, while men, women and young people searched through the thicket of foliage near the creek. Lucille had gathered all of the younger children and taken them to her house to tend, freeing their parents for the search. Sherry, Paul and Roger firmly held one another's hands in fear of losing another friend. Each felt a personal loss with Tillie's absence and wanted to be able to play with her again soon.

Joe Peterson, Ralph Stewart and George Evans, all with fishing waders, were waist deep in the frigid current. Each man held onto a rope extended from the two banks and were slowly working their way downstream.

An icy shiver shot through both women as they approached the scene. Disbelief racked Gwen's mind. This couldn't be happening, not to her little Tillie. She couldn't be caught among boulders and debris in that icy water, her body void of life. No! Her mind echoed refusal again and again. This is just a nightmare! This isn't really happening, it's a dream and I'll awake in the morning and everything will be as usual.

Susan put an arm around her friend's waist. Both women seemed to go into a shock as reality engulfed them. They merged in with their friends and neighbors in the hunt for the lost child. The search continued long into the night.

No trace of the little girl was found. Shortly after mid-night, when Gwen was returning to the house to check on her mother, she saw Emma bent over Matilda. Alarmed at her mother's condition, Gwen quickened her steps, but upon closer scrutiny, she realized the women were deep in conversation. Before she could reach the porch, she watched Emma wheel around and run into the tool shed. It was only a second or two until she emerged and disappeared into the dark. She did not join those hunting in the region of the creek, but faded into the black shadow of trees in the direction of the railroad tracks.

Tillie's Tale Continues

illie paused with her tale, shivered in the snow that had begun a hour earlier, took a deep breath, then continued.

When I reached the lane, I thought I had better cut the screams and hide. Granny was so far behind that I couldn't see her. I kept running and as I passed the creek, my hat bounced off my head and went into the water, but I didn't dare to take time to fetch it, I just kept going. I raced through the corral and the manure to the barn. No one was in sight. Up the ladder to the hayloft I went.

I crawled over to the far, far corner and pulled loose hay all around me, then one, last bunch over the top. Me and the entire corner were concealed with dried alfalfa, but I had several little air holes and a peek-hole so I could see the yard between the barn and the house.

Quietly, I waited. There could be no more tears or sobs; no noise of any kind, or I would be found.

Loud voices came from the yard. Lots of them. The whole family and Granny P. starting calling my name. Of course, I knew enough to stay put and not answer, but I did peek out of the hole in the side of the loft. They were looking all over for me, but I didn't move. This went on all day. Other people came to help look for me, then it was time to milk the cows and do the evening chores. I could hear Leland and John in the stable, feeding and milking the cows. The rest of the family was still looking for me.

It started to get dark and cold. Other people came to help look for me. Clay Oliver was over near the ditch, talking to Daddy, I guess he had come to take me to jail. His horse and buggy were tied to the corral fence by several other buggies. There were also a half a dozen cars parked in the yard.

People were scattered all over, calling my name. They were even looking up and down the creek. I was sure in a lot of trouble. Half the town had come to help Clay take me to jail, even my own family was going to send me away.

I could see Mama standing on the grass. She had both hands up to her face. There was that red face and tears again. Susan went over to her and they started hugging and crying. Even Roger was there. Somehow, I knew he would turn against me. Then Sherry and her parents came into the yard. Well, that little tattle-tale, she probably blamed everything onto me, cause she wasn't in jail. Lucille came and took Sherry and the rest of the kids and left.

After dark, they had torches and were looking downstream of the creek. Joe Peterson and some other men were in the creek wading and feeling around for something. Maybe they were looking for the money. I fell asleep for a little while, but I could still hear them. They weren't in the yard now. The house was all lit up like a Christmas tree. I couldn't stay in the loft for the rest of my life, there was only one thing left. I knew what I had to do.

Very quietly, I crawled out of my cover, and climbed down the ladder. I was careful not to be seen as I slipped back through the corral and climbed between the poles of the fence, then headed over toward the railroad tracks in the opposite direction from the search.

It was scary to go into the thicket alone at night, so I ran fast after I crossed the tracks. It didn't matter if I made lots of noise after that 'cause Clay and the others wouldn't be able to hear me. After a while, I saw a dark figure up ahead of me. It was you, but I could also hear someone coming behind me. I guessed it was your friend.

Tillie rested from her tale, became quiet and took a deep breath, exhaling audibility. The sound cracked the silence that had suddenly appeared moments earlier. She gave another sigh as her eyes probed the tramps in uncertainty.

Norman continued to watch the child, but didn't speak. Her

story had clearly stirred his mind, leaving his questions concerning her satisfied. However, he was now torn between the need of the child to return the money and his own need for survival during the freezing, winter months ahead.

The three years he had lived in the open with no shelter seemed like centuries. His future without the money would be much more bleak than her's. If he kept the money, it would be enough to provide food and a room for the winter, something like a dream come true.

The large woman hadn't moved, nor had she spoken during the entire tale, she had held her distance, with her alert, keen eyes fixed on the other two. Her mien seemed to be one of observation, still, Norman was unsure of her involvement.

Early dawn was starting to break. The freight would be passing shortly. Thick snow clouds covered the sky, leaving the soon to be sunrise dimmed in the gray, morning hour. Max Smith's rooster began his morning alarm call, and soon several other roosters, closer into town, echoed his crow.

An early-season, light snow was fluttering through the trees. Almost immediately, it changed to a heavier storm quickly covering the earth with a white skirt. Visibility was becoming hazy.

"Please give me the box, so I can take the money back." The girl's words traveled through the falling flakes.

"Ah said Ah ain't got no box. Ya got yer wires crossed. Must ta been that other bunch what took the box."

"No! You've got the box! I put it with the coat! I'll go to jail if I don't take it back and besides, I don't want my life to be full of stinky things. I want to clean it up."

Blast the darn girl! Why did she have to rattle on about making things right? Why couldn't she just drop it? Had God sent her to prick his conscience? Heaven knows he had tried, tried hard to be honest even when he was starving and cold. He had to steal now and then, not big things, but enough to keep going.

Norman didn't answer, but looked at the woman. In the dim morning light, her features began to break through. He saw a pleasant face that held a stern facade, appropriate for the present situation. Her dress, as much as he could see, although faded, was clean, starched and ironed. The long coat, covering her figure, was of good quality, but aged and threadbare. She still clutched the wrench in her right hand. He surmised it was for protection and not to be used in an offensive.

A moment later he asked. "How do Ah know ya two ain't workin' tagether, ta do me outa what's mine? Who are ya anyway?" His voice raised, he nodded at the woman, realizing she was a nice-looking woman and close to his same age.

Tillie, concerned with her own plight regarding the box, had forgotten about the woman. She turned, and in a surprised voice, exclaimed, "Emma!"

Emma walked across the space to where Tillie was still perched on the rock. Reaching out, her left arm encircled the girl's frame in a protective manner, the wrench remained in her other hand ready for action if need be.

"Everything's going to be okay, dear. Don't you worry your little head. Everything's fine."

Watching the two, Norman's countenance reflected a softening. "If Ah give ya the box, what about me? Ah'll be out in the cold with nuthin'. Ya two don't know what it's like with no job or home ta go ta." He paused momentarily, then smiled at the pair. "If Ah give ya the box, cain Ah keep the coat ta help keep me warm?"

"No. I gotta take the coat back to Mr. Sorenson," replied Tillie, shuddering at the thought of facing the school principal. She was more frightened of facing the menacing Mr. Sorenson than anything else ahead of her. In her mind, it was even scarier than going to jail.

"You can come with me to my house and we'll see if my daddy will give you his coat. He's nice about sharing. His coat's not new like this one, but it'll keep you warm and my mama would even give you something to eat."

At the thought of someone giving him a coat, Norman's eyes suddenly became misty, making his vision even more foggy than it had been in the heavy falling snow. With a quick shake of his head, he thrust the moving emotion aside as if it were some deadly enemy. He couldn't afford such softness. Memories of an absence of kindness these past years darkened his mind. There had only been a handful of kind acts or any sympathetic treatment since he'd been on the road. Time and time again, he'd felt as if his heart were dragging the ground from the hurt. The probability of even a gift of an old coat seemed impossible. No, he'd never seen such kindness handed out. This could be a trap or the child believed in fairy tales, probably the latter. Still…

He looked at the girl bundled in Horace Sorenson's coat, he had developed a nagging fondness for the little chit, while she had related her tale. She no longer appeared odd-looking, but almost like he imagined a child-angel to look, one that had wandered through a murky corral.

———

Norman looked in the direction of the tracks. It was nearing time for the east-bound freight to be passing through. The snow continued to thicken, building a deep layer of ground covering and casting a dim view of the town beyond the tracks. Echo of the calls from the searchers could no longer be heard. It appeared those pursuing in the hunt had settled into the hopelessness of finding Tillie. He assumed most had returned to their homes, weary of heart and spirit at not finding the missing child.

However, at the Swensen farm, there were still several men along with the family, persisting until now, not willing to give up until Tillie's remains were recovered. John and Leland, also reluctant to end their efforts, were slowly walking toward the barn, ready to do the morning feeding and milking. Charolette and Beverly, exhausted, had returned to the house several hours earlier. Granny P., determined of mind, had been unwilling to go to her own home and had fallen asleep on Gwen's bed. Tillie's parents, amid the falling winter flakes, were offering their thanks and appreciation to neighbors at their leave. All, laid low with sorrow and fatigue, had little to say as they left the Swensen farm.

Joe Peterson, Clay Oliver, Wilbert Brown the school janitor, along with Horace Sorenson were over near the creek. They too, were bringing their efforts to an end and preparing to go home.

During most of the long day and part of the night, Joe, Clay and Wilbert had concentrated on the depths of the creek, while Horace, whose expertise was in telling others what to do, had occupied a huge rock during the entire search. He had settled himself on the lofty, white stone, aloof the entire time, but had contributed many words, telling those beneath him what to do. In his mind, these simple farmers would have been at a loss without his wise guidance. In reality, they had merely gone about the hunt, ignoring the cocky creature perched above, as he spewed his words into the cold, unhearing atmosphere.

The men's attention was drawn to the railroad tracks and the freight in the far distance, the blasting whistle burst forth it's warning of approach. As if not to be outdone by this boastful sound, the roaring engine, with the beacon light shining ahead through the dim morning air, sped down the snow-covered tracks. Nearer and nearer, the iron vehicle came, pulling the laden cars, the wheels meeting in kinship with icy, cold tracks.

———————

In the thicket, the three, drab figures also turned their attention to the thunderous roar. Louder and louder came the sound of the piercing whistle, almost splitting their eardrums.

Amid the clamor of stirred wind and noise, Norman glanced at the fast moving train and his last opportunity to escape with the money. This was a vehicle to a warmer climate and a better life. He quickly looked at the woman, then at Tillie and smiled. In a soft voice, he muttered, "I'm sorry, really, I am."

The two, anxious to get the matter settled properly, relaxed their stance and smiled back at him. He just stood there, peering into their faces, his smile transfixed, his eyes radiating a kind, understanding gaze.

Suddenly, he whirled around and bolted past Emma, knocking her off balance, then, with a hasty push of his left hand, he pushed her onto her back. Emma bumped Tillie and she too met the ground. Recovering themselves into sitting positions, they watched Norman make a mad dash for the fast moving freight, slipping and stumbling along the covered path. He tripped over a fallen, protruding tree limb, fell nearly to the ground, then recovered his balance and ran for the train. As he was trying to regain his footing, he dropped the sack he had been carrying. He didn't stop to retrieve the fallen object, but continued to make haste for the iron horse, knowing full well this was his only chance.

Emma and Tillie, still on the ground, watched Norman run alongside an open boxcar, his legs faltering on the slick incline to the tracks, as he tried desperately to reach for the iron bar on the door. Unable to grasp the fixture, the car sped past him. He did not slacken his pace, but reached again for the next car. Again his missed the bar and was forced to keep his now steady gait. A second later, another car passed him, this time the door was bolted shut. He kept running alongside the locked vehicle, again slipping and stumbling in the snow. The next two cars were also closed. Closed boxcars clattered along the tracks, then one with an open door was along his side.

As he grabbed for the iron bar, his foot met with a rock jutting up through the snow, and he lost his balance and fell. Emma and Tillie watched in horror as he dropped head first underneath the car. While he kept a firm grip on the bar, his body did not meet with the racing wheels, but floundered as he slowly worked himself up alongside the car and then hoisted himself in through the door.

He stood, turned and looked at the two figures in the thicket, growing smaller and smaller as he moved out of their lives and onto supposedly better times. The stark emptiness that entered his stomach and spread to his body, then filtered into his limbs was not the hunger he often felt from lack of food, but was much more piercing, an emotion of a profound sense of loss, something that he had not experienced in a long time. He shook himself, trying to rid himself of the unwelcome sensation.

Emma's Words

Upon seeing Norman safe in the car, both the girl and woman expelled their breaths, happy that he was not crushed beneath the rushing, powerful, round jaws.

Emma was the first to her feet. Giving Tillie, who was now crying, a hand, she said, "He dropped something in the snow, maybe it's the box of money. Let's go see."

Tillie wiped her eyes and gave Emma a shy smile as they started following Norman's tracks. The heavy snow was rapidly covering his hastily made footprints. They shuffled along his trail as best they could, uncovering anything slightly raised along the trail.

Tillie was the first to see it. Calling to Emma, "Here it is, over here." She ran to the snow-covered article now hiding under mother nature's winter shirts and immediately began to dig beneath the white blanket. It was the sack with a few, hardened, left-over, Halloween cookies, a can of fish and the cigar box. Eagerly, she lifted the lid. To her dismay, it was empty. Mr. Brough's money was gone.

Tired, cold and hungry, this was more than Tillie could handle. She sat down in the snow and began to cry.

"Now I can never go home," she wailed.

Emma stooped in the snow and faced the child, their eyes meeting. Emma's held a reassurance, while Tillie's betrayed a disappointment mingled with fright.

Emma spoke, "Yes you can. Now, let's go home. Your mother and father are worried sick about you. They love you and want to help you. Tillie, you have a good family and they'll always help you, no matter what. I want you to always remember that."

They trudged through the trees, leaving fresh footprints in the fallen snow. Emma's steps were much shorter than usual, while Tillie's tracks showed a shuffling in the oversized boots. Horace Sorenson's coat, still draped around the girl, dredged their trail with the hem, making their path slightly covered and a little wider.

Tillie said, "I really thought he was going to return the box and I feel sad that he didn't, but what I feel the worst about is that he made a bad choice just like I did, only he's decided not to clean up his mess. Now he'll never know if our town would have helped him. Maybe he could have even taken a bath and maybe be a daddy for you."

At the child's reasoning, Emma's jaw dropped followed by a humorous chuckle. Her thoughts were that Tillie could certainly use a lesson in match-making. First, it was Joe Peterson, at least fifteen years her junior, now it was an unbathed, unemployed hobo that lived with the word ain't. Still, he did have a nice face and a good scrubbing, hair cut and clean clothes sometimes brought about a miracle, but then, there's the word ain't. Emma cast these thoughts from her mind as if she were a fisherman tossing a small fish back into the river.

"That's right Tillie. He'll never know what might have been, nor what blessings he could have had by making the right choice. When we humans make wrong choices, we fail to know the wonderful blessings, from Heavenly Father, that we are missing by traveling the wrong road, and when we do make wrong choices, most of us refuse to recognize and admit it. You did, and you are well on your way to living the way Heavenly Father wants you to."

Hearing this, Tillie beamed with pride, but lost some of the full meaning when Emma continued. "You have a beautiful soul." Tillie wondered what the soles of her boots had to do with beauty. She knew they were well-worn, with holes in the toes and one even had a hole in the bottom, and the cardboard that had been inserted inside was also worn through. Now the snow was making her feet cold. The thought came to her that Emma must be affected by the cold.

Emma went on talking. "I know Max Smith would have hired

him to help out on his farm. Max is old and needs the help. The tramp could have had room and board and maybe a few extra dollars each month. That would have helped the Smith's and him until this depression is over." She paused, glanced down at Tillie and continued. "Yes. One of the saddest things in life is what might have been if we would just travel the high road."

"I'm scared for all the trouble I caused. I'm glad me and Sherry helped some of the tramps, cause they sure needed it, but I'm sorry I stole things to do it. Now I don't quite know how to make everything right. How am I ever going to pay Mr. Brough all that money back? I don't think Sherry and Paul and Roger will ever play with me again."

"Yes they will. All your friends are worried that something terrible has happened to you. They'll probably want to play with you as soon as possible."

They walked a few steps in silence, then Emma trying to reassure Tillie said, "It's wonderful that you realize you made a mistake and are trying to make everything right. You won't be sent to jail. You're too young to be fully responsible. Your daddy and mama will help you fix everything. They are the ones that are responsible for the things you do and will be until you get a little older. They love you very much and want to help, and Tillie, I hope you'll always think of me as a friend and not think of me as the spanking lady."

Tillie turned her head slightly upward and blinked as a snowflake caught her lash, then she flashed Emma a big smile.

The Reunions

*G*wen was the first to see the two figures trudging through the deepening snow, wending their way toward the house. Only the Swensens, Wilbert Brown and Horace Sorenson were in the yard. Clay Oliver and Joe Peterson had just left several minutes earlier in Clay's buggy. Disheartened and discouraged, Henry was entering the barn to give his sons a hand with the morning chores. Horace and Wilbert were conversing over by the gate on the far side of the yard.

Mother and daughter ran to each other, Gwen in long strides, while Tillie's were somewhat hampered by the dragging coat. Gwen swept her little girl up into her arms, whirled circular in the snow, while she covered Tillie with hugs and kisses.

"Oh, sweetheart, you're alive!" she exclaimed, tears running down her cheeks. "Henry! Look Henry! She's over here!"

Henry turned, not believing his eyes, stood mesmerized, blinked, blinked again; he flew through the snow to where they were embraced. Emma, witnessing the exciting reunion, basked in their happiness. Henry took his daughter from Gwen, squeezed her tightly, then held her close to his chest and was about to speak when Tillie said, "Daddy, it was me that took the money from the bank."

"I know, sweetheart. Sherry told us what you girls had been doing."

"She tattled-taled?"

"No. No. When we couldn't find you, I questioned her about what you girls had been doing. She was trying to be helpful, so we could find you. We were frightened something terrible had happened to you. Where on earth have you been?" Then, not waiting for an answer, he added quickly, "You must never, never do anything like that again. Promise me!"

"I promise. Cross my heart, hope to die if I should ever tell a lie." While crossing her heart, she rattled the chant the children used to promise truth.

Tillie put a little hand on each side of her Daddy's face, looked straight into his eyes and said, "Sherry and I took all those things to try and help the hungry tramps, and one tramp found all the stuff we had hidden, even all the rest of the money. Then he ran away on the train. He wouldn't give the money back."

She paused to collect herself, then went on. "Daddy, I tried and tried to get the money back from the tramp, so I could give it back to Mr. Brough, but he ran away with it. He said he needed it cause he don't have no food or no home. Daddy, I'm sorry." Then she started to cry.

"Hush, hush. Don't cry sweetheart, I've already talked to Mr. Brough. We'll pay him back a little bit each month. He said we could do it on a loan. We're just glad you're okay." As he said this, Gwen reached over and wiped her daughter's tears.

"This afternoon, we'll go around to all the people you took things from, you can tell them you're sorry and we'll arrange to square everything with them. I'll help you. Sherry said she wanted to make things right too. Maybe she and her daddy can go with us if they want to do it that way, but it's important that everyone is repaid for the things you girls took. That's the right thing to do."

Little arms encircled Henry's neck, followed by a kiss on the cheek.

Out of the corner of her eye, Tillie saw Horace Sorenson strutting in the direction of his car. Wilbert Brown had left and was driving down the lane in his car. Climbing down from her father's arms, she slowly made her way toward the man, the one she feared most in all the world. The hem of his new jacket was still dragging behind her.

Emma and her parents followed, but remained a few steps away. Henry, anxious for his little girl and watchful of Sorenson's reaction, moved closer to his daughter and waited.

Horace's jaw dropped when he spied his coat moving through the snow as if by some invisible means. At first, Tillie's head was inconspicuous because of the poor visibility. For a fleeting second, Horace experienced an eerie, ghostly sensation, then he saw the odd, little head with the sparse, wet hair slicked down against her scalp. His mind began working, everything was now falling into place.

The hot-headed, school principal's contorted face turned a fiery red, his vision blurred with emotion, then he began to shake, while an angry numbness spread through his body.

He shouted in a loud, quivering voice. "Why you little brat! It was you all the time. Look what you've done to my new coat. You'll pay for this! Mark my words! Your dad will rue the day you were born!" Then he shouted in Henry's direction, shaking his fist in the air. "You'll pay for this Henry Swensen! You'll pay for this!"

Both Henry and Gwen, drained from their ordeal of the last fifteen hours, along with knowing of their daughter's misdeeds, waited in silence.

Tillie took off the coat and held it up to Mr. Sorenson. Grabbing it, he began brushing the snow, wet leaves and mud from the mackinaw, then abruptly stopped brushing and seized the child's arm. He lifted her out of the snow and began to shake her, all the time spewing profanities at the little girl.

In two quick strides, Henry's strong, working hands were gripping Horace's collar at the front of his neck. Horace lost his hold of Tillie's limb. Falling into the snow, she hurriedly regained her footing in time to hear her father's hissing words between clenched teeth.

Henry laid strong, clear emphasis on each word as he warned, "I appreciate your help in our search for Tillie, but if you ever so much as touch this child or any one of my other kids in or out of school, you'll regret the day you ever heard of this town." Henry released his hold, giving the man a slight shove, then took a step backward, still glaring menacingly at the principal.

Horace stumbled, trying to regain his balance and was about to attack Henry. Sensibility warned him that his soft, unworked body was no match for Henry's muscled frame.

He was still livid with rage, when Emma stepped forward, putting her hand on his arm to speak. The angry man shook her hand free, still, Emma persisted, "Horace! Get control of yourself! Stop acting like a child and listen to this little girl, you may learn something!"

The firmness of Emma's hand invaded his raging thoughts. His mind whirled. Learn something from this dirty, little, ugly tom-boy? Never! These stupid country people could never teach him anything!

Horace looked at Emma, the most domineering woman in town, she was the only person he felt was anywhere near his equal. With great effort to control himself, he begrudgingly turned to Tillie, his face still red and his body shaking with rage. She could talk, but his mind was set on refusal to listen.

In a timid voice, Tillie said, "Mr. Sorenson, I'm sorry I took your coat. I hope you'll forgive me. I thought the tramps needed it more than you did cause you got a job to earn money and they don't have nothing. They get real cold cause they don't have no place to go. You've got a warm house. Besides, the way Bess Hussy was keeping you warm. I thought you don't deserve a warm house or a family."

Hearing this, Emma almost lost her teeth. Quickly clamping her hand over her mouth, she silently wished she could afford better fitting dentures.

The revelation of he and Bess Hussy gave him slight pause, but only for a moment, as Tillie continued. "Now I'm trying to make things right cause I want a nice, clean life, one that I can be proud of. Maybe you should clean up the stinky part of your's too."

Henry and Gwen shifted uncomfortably. They hadn't wanted to know of Horace's infidelity. Neither would they ever repeat what they had just heard, mainly out of respect for Priscilla Sorenson. Why add extra hurt?

Horace turned and stomped through the snow, muttering under his breath. When he reached his car, he shouted something indiscernible. His words, intemperate, were lost amid the white flakes in the heartless storm.

Tears erupted from Tillie. Emma, still anxious to give reassurance to the girl, said, "Tillie, Horace Sorenson is traveling down a one-way street in the wrong direction. You've tried to make things right, but he is the only one that can determine if there will be stink, as you call it, in his life. You can't change him, no one can except himself. Do you understand that?"

Tillie nodded as Gwen lifted her daughter into her arms and wrapping her own coat around the snow-covered child, said, "Let's go in the house and get some breakfast. The family will be excited to know that you are home. Emma, come in and have some breakfast with us. Then, you and Tillie can tell us everything."

Henry, wanting to calm his irate emotions after his confrontation with Horace, walked briskly to the barn to tell John and Leland that their sister was safely home. Gwen, Emma and Tillie made their way down the path to the house, anxious to spread the glad news to Granny P. and the girls.

Granny had built a roaring fire in the cook stove and was in the middle of preparing breakfast. Tillie burst through the kitchen door and ran to her granny. Matilda was so taken by surprise, she gasped for air, her right hand raced to her heart, her left hand steadied her frame as she lowered herself into the wooden rocker.

"Oh Tillie! Tillie! You're okay," she sobbed as her granddaughter climbed onto her lap to give her a hug.

"Granny, I love you and I'm sorry that I upset you. Let's still be friends."

"Yes! Yes! We're still friends and I love you too," Granny cried as she clutched her grand-daughter to her breast.

Charolette and Beverly, asleep on the couch in the living room, were awakened by the commotion. Immediately, they jumped out of bed and scampered into the kitchen to join the happy reunion.

The sound of footsteps rang from the wooden porch. The door burst open, and John and Leland rushed into the kitchen to welcome their youngest sister home. Henry loomed in the doorway. He had banished the thought of Horace Sorenson from his mind as he basked in the happy reunion of his family.

A Lesson Learned

*M*eanwhile, Horace Sorenson cranked his motor and headed down the lane toward town. He hadn't gone far, when Clay Oliver's slow traveling buggy was blocking the one- lane drive.

Clay and Joe Peterson, hats pulled low on their heads as shields against the cold elements, were both hunched forward on the seat of the trap. Horace pulled his vehicle directly behind them and commandingly blasted the horn of the automobile. The horses shied, as the harsh, loud noise pierced their sensitive ears, pulling the buggy off to the side of the road. Clay firmly gripped the reins and spoke to the team in a calm voice, then regained control of the animals.

Horace drove to the side of the buggy and stepped from his vehicle. Before his feet even touched the snow, he launched into his tirade of Tillie's return and confession of her evil mischief. The more he vented his spleen, the more his voice trembled, and the more his voice trembled, the more his body shook and his face grew to a darkish, red hue.

Clay and Joe, both relieved and delighted with the news of Tillie's return, released their pent-up stress and concern for the child immediately. Broad smiles appeared on their faces as Horace wailed his woe of the corrupt child. They held no empathy for the raving man. Clay was having a difficult time to keep from laughing. Joe just smirked, with little patience for the performance before them.

This enraged Horace even more. He demanded that Clay arrest Tillie for the bloody threats she had made to him and also for the theft of his coat. He wanted justice. The pent-up hatred that he had harbored for his inferiors oozed from every pore.

Finally, Joe interrupted the raging Horace and said, "Horace! You can't blame Tillie or any of these kids around here for what they do to try and aggravate you. They are just returning what you have given to them. Dislike!" The last word was emphasized in a harsh, loud voice. Joe continued, "That's what you've taught down at that school and thanks to the good Lord,the other teachers down there aren't like you. They've got their acts together. Now, why don't you just go home, forget about all this nonsense and clean up your own life? You've got a lot to be thankful for. Personally, I'm glad those little girls took my long johns, maybe some poor ol' guy stuck out in the cold is a little bit warmer right now."

Joe's words were lost on the principal. Mr. Sorenson's spirit held no comprehension, but Joe continued, "Maybe, we adults needed a lesson in helping some of the more unfortunate. I know everyone in this town is having a hard time making a go of it. But we could easily donate a little each week to help those with nothing. Two five-year-olds tried to do what we grownups should've been doing all along."

Horace, disgusted with the two men, returned to his car and drove home.

As the morning drew on, the entire community became aware of Tillie's safe return. Slowly, the details of her escapade were related, mostly by way of Lucille Evans' information network; her mouth.

———

Later that morning, at Sunday services, the community gathered together and unitedly gave thanks for the safe return of Tillie Swensen. The children in the nursery class all viewed Tillie as some kind of a heroine. That is, all except Burt and Bart Hussy, both of which shifted uncomfortably in their seats when the teacher commented that her black eye and the cut on her cheek were almost better.

Most of the citizenry reacted much the same as Clay Oliver and Joe Peterson; happy and relieved that Tillie was alive and unharmed. Then the humor of it all brought a few chuckles at their failure to see what was going on beneath their own eyes.

After, a feeling of shame and regret penetrated their souls for having neglected those poor, which were many.

Within two weeks, Lucille Evans, along with Mabel Stewart and Emma Olsen, organized a soup line for the hungry. Nearly every family in town contributed an item for the pot. It worked out that only a couple of vegetables each week was all that was needed from each family.

With the exception of the bank, where it was necessary that the money be repaid, and Mr. Sorenson's belief that he had been severely wronged, everyone was more than happy to have been a contributor to the needy. However, at each home, when Tillie and Sherry faced their victims to try and clear up their stinky mess, the girls were strictly admonished to never, never again, take anything that didn't belong to them without permission. Both girls solemnly promised they would make every effort to be honest, trustworthy girls. The girls were anxious to put the whole matter behind them and move onto other new and adventurous things.

They were also relieved that it would be almost a whole year before they would enter the first grade and have to face the menacing Mr. Sorenson.

Epilogue

November 5, 1935

*H*enry Swensen let the newspaper fall to the floor. He had spent most of the day feeding and putting dry bedding straw in the sheds for his stock. Wet and cold, he had returned to the house for a temporary reprieve. Now, he rested his head against the back of the wooden rocker, stretched his stocking feet out toward the heat of the kitchen stove and was about to close his eyes, when he saw the lone figure bent low, to shield against the thick flakes of white, making his way to the front gate.

There had been a two-day lull in the storm, however, the heavy snow had resumed soon after breakfast. Hopefully, the weather would soon revert back to the normal fall pattern.

The man, tall and scantily dressed for the icy snow, made his way through the gate and yard, up the steps and onto the back porch.

Moisture had collected on the glass, casting a dim picture, which made the man indistinguishable as he passed the frosty pane. Henry's interest ignited immediately. Even with the blurry picture through the window, Henry knew he had never seen the man before.

Gwen had just finished her weekly ironing and was folding the board for storage. A pot of chili slowly simmered on the back of the Monarch cook stove. They would have wheat bread, chili and a dish of bottled peaches for supper.

Since her escapade in the thicket, Tillie, now more content to linger near her parents, was sitting at the kitchen table trying to learn her numbers. Her head bent low in concentration,she was oblivious to her surroundings, as she meticulously tried to recreate the numbers that Beverly had written for her the previous evening. Her older siblings would soon be arriving from school to complete the family gathering.

This tranquil scene was disrupted by a firm knock on the door.

Putting her iron on the pantry shelf, Gwen closed the door and gave Henry a quick glance, "I'll get it," then went to the door. Tillie, still absorbed in the numbers, was uninterested by the intrusion of any visitor. Henry's interest piqued, rose from the chair, and falling in behind his wife, also went to the door.

Turning the knob, she stepped aside and held the door to it's full capacity. Flurries from the storm rushed past the stranger, into the room. Amid the falling flakes stood a shabbily dressed man. His clothes were soaked from the fall of the wet snow, while ice crystals clung to the outermost parts of his ragged clothes. Upon seeing Gwen, he removed his hat, that too was drenched, as was his unkept, straggly hair. Holding his cap with both hands at the front of his waist, he started to speak. Then Henry appeared, his head towering above Gwen's.

"Are yeh Henry and Gwen Swensen, little Tillie's daddy and mummy?" Both nodded in unison. "Can Ah talk ta ya a bit?"

"Please come in." Gwen motioned him inside, while Henry stepped back, allowing the man to pass. Norman was struck by Gwen's attractive looks. His first impression was Tillie held no resemblance to her pretty mother. Closer observance brought a change to this idea. The olive coloring was the same, Tillie's eyes were more like her father's. Long, beautiful hair, the desire of Tillie's heart, was lacking, but Tillie's was beginning to grow. This would bring much of the physical beauty with it, which Tillie so much desired. His concluding thought on this subject was; Tillie, your turn will come.

With concern for this newcomer, who was obviously one of those riding the rails and showed distinct signs of hunger along with his freezing condition, Gwen reached out for his elbow and said, "Come over near the stove. You're wet and cold. It's more comfortable by the fire."

When Norman entered the room, the rank odor that Tillie had become familiar with several days earlier, rushed in with him. The warmth of the room intensified the stinging, caustic smell. Tillie sniffed, then took her eyes from the paper and exclaimed in a loud voice, "You came back!"

He turned to face Tillie, but backed closer to the warmth of the stove. "Yeh. Ah come back. Ah thought about what ya said about a stinky life. Ya kind of got ta me."

Gwen walked to the cupboard, removed a soup bowl from the shelf and began to fill it with warm chili, then set it on the table.

The tramp hesitated, looked at the food, then turned to Henry who had remained quiet. "Ah'm sorry ta trouble ya two, but Ah need ta talk ta ya a bit, then Ah'll be on ma way. Ah just couldn't bring maself ta spend any of the money. So, Ah brung it back." He lifted a wad of currency from the inside pocket of his jacket and handed it to Henry. Henry took the wet currency, looked at it, bewildered by the tramp's honesty. Gwen too, was happily shaken by his action.

"All Ah took is here. Ah didn't spend none of it. And Ah'm sorry fer all the trouble Ah caused."

"Why?" questioned Henry. "What made you decide to return it, when it's obvious you are in dire need?"

"It bothered me all the way ta Denver. Ah got inta one of the soup lines and ate, then I hopped the first freight that Ah could ta come back. Ah had to, after what Tillie said about a stinky life."

Gwen sliced several pieces of bread and poured some milk into a glass. "You sit here and eat, then we'll fill the tub in the pantry with warm water. You'll have privacy in there. I've got the kettle full. You can soak some of the cold out of your bones. I've just finished ironing. You can wear these when you get out." She picked up one of Henry's shirts and a pair of mended overalls, along with some socks and underclothing.

Henry looked at his wife. They locked eyes as they often did when they mentally communicated. He knew of the stranger's need, and that for now, he would have to do with two sets of work clothes, one on and one off. Neither he nor Gwen could, in good conscience, keep all and not share with this cold and weary man. They were joined together in their feelings of his need.

The man timidly approached the table, pulled out a chair and lowered himself to the seat. He did not immediately lift the filled spoon to his mouth, but quietly bowed his head for several seconds, as if to give thanks for the unexpected kindness he was now receiving. Tillie's parents, both deeply moved by his humble action, also bowed their heads and gave thanks that they had enough to share. As he raised his head and began his meal, their eyes suddenly became misty as they witnessed the man relish in his feast.

Tillie, unaware of the sacred moment of appreciation and thanks, went to the coat rack on the wall, took down her little winter coat, then rummaged through the wooden box by the back door for a pair of rubber boots.

Gwen looked at her daughter, "Where are you going in this weather?"

"To Emma's."

"Why?"

"To tell her the tramp came back."

"Tillie!" Gwen's voice held a note of disapproval with Tillie's answer. "Tillie, this gentleman has a name."

Norman, extremely surprised at being referred to as a gentleman, whirled around and waited to clear his last bite of food. He had been called many things the past few years, but never in all his life had he ever been called a gentleman.

To Gwen, though his speech and dress spoke otherwise, his intense honesty under his adverse conditions, his prayer of thanks and his manners since he entered their home, classed him, in her mind, above any ordinary man. To her, he was indeed a gentleman.

Norman finished chewing the beans that were in his mouth, looked at Henry, then Gwen and rested his eyes on Tillie and in a serious tone, said, "Ma name is Norman Bello."

Tillie's come-back was, "I'll tell Emma that." And in a blaze of excitement, she hurried out the door, anxious to get to Emma's house with what she thought was some promising news. News, which she hoped might someday effect Emma and the tramp.

Tillie didn't hear her mother's words as she called out to her, "Remember, Roger asked to come and play with you at four o'clock."